CHAPTER ONE

The dragon was coming. Scarlet and gold, its mouth as wide as an open window, it swayed slowly down the centre of the road. The crowd cheered. Low Hee cheered. This was why he'd waited all morning in the sun.

Low Hee and some of his mates from school were messing around in the crowds, scooting between legs, laughing when people nearly toppled. Because it was the last day of the New Year celebrations, their victims laughed back. Old women handed them *laisee* envelopes, red packets stuffed with coins, and everyone tossed sweets at everyone else.

Now, he realized, he was too far back. Cymbals and bells, tumblers and jugglers came first in the procession but the dragon would soon be in view. All Low Hee could see were the heads in front. He dropped to his knees and wriggled his shoulders between two sets of silk-draped legs. He would be at the front of the crowd in seconds.

"Come here!"

Low Hee's grandmother had him by the sleeve of his coat. Her face was rather grim. He stopped his wriggling.

"I wasn't doing anything..." he mumbled, quickly swallowing a mouthful of chocolate bar.

7

"And the dragon is coming!" He was longing to see it. But his grandmother's hold on his sleeve was as tight as her expression. There was nothing else he could do but follow her through the wide portals of the temple.

The gigantic statue of the Buddha dominated a whole wall of the temple. It smiled down with a mocking leer. Low Hee longed to poke its huge stomach. He could almost believe that his finger would not hit hard, cold metal, but disappear into the softness of fat and skin.

Just by the entrance, a fortune-teller sat behind a small table of ornate ivory. He was so ancient, the skin of his hairless head was as pale and smooth as his table. Behind him, hangings dangled from the wall of the temple proclaiming his skills in divination. A cluster of people had gathered round him, plucking out straws of differing lengths from vases decorated with gilded serpents.

Low's grandmother, Ee Tsang, was talking to the wizened old man. She always had her fortune told when she had any important decision to make, but she did not usually include her grandson. Low moved closer, fascinated despite his longing to see the dragon.

"What is the boy's age?" the fortune-teller was saying.

"He is nearly twelve years old," Ee Tsang replied. She seated herself comfortably, at the request of the teller. Low stood beside her, his lips half parted and warm breath moving fast through his teeth. They were talking about him. His future.

"What is the problem that besets him?"

"I wish to know if my grandson will take a long voyage."

"Grandmother..." Low Hee began. But he was quickly silent when Ee Tsang gave him a sharp look. Low knew it would be disrespectful to ask for an explanation. He was only a boy; he had no right to question why his grandmother wanted his fortune told, however much he longed to ask. He stayed quite still until Ee Tsang raised a silk-covered arm and motioned him to pick a straw.

Low Hee's fingers hovered over the porcelain vase. His gaze caught the old man's and, for just a moment, Low looked into the rheumy eyes. It was as though he could see his own destiny in their wet depths, without ever hearing it spoken out loud. He let his finger rest on a single straw. He drew it out and passed it to the man.

"The journey is a certain one," squeaked the soothsayer. "The journey is a long one. It will take the boy to a foreign place. There he will reside. He will not return."

Ee Tsang's head suddenly bobbed down on to her finely embroidered New Year clothes. She shut her eyes tightly but not before the wrinkled skin around them had become wet. Low saw her fingers work around themselves in her lap. The knuckles were white. He'd never before seen his grandmother lose her self-possession in public.

Embarrassed, he turned his attention to the grinning Buddha. Now he knew why that grin mocked him. His head swam with new thoughts. His lips silently formed the words, "My father".

Low knew he ought to be able to remember his father's face. He'd been four and a half when his parents had left Malaysia and he could remember plenty of other things that happened when he was four, including the trip across the Straits to the orang-utan enclosure. He knew he'd been taken by his parents as a last treat before they left for England, but although he could clearly picture the apes as they chased each other over the ground and into the high trees, he couldn't remember his father at all, or much about his mother.

If he struggled, however, he could bring an image into his mind of an almond lady. An almond-shaped face with almond-coloured skin. Even the smell of her was almond. He could recollect bringing his lips to a soft, sweet-scented cheek, and words, coming through a mist, the last words she must have spoken to him.

"Your honourable grandmother is to be your mother now. Esteem her highly, Low Hee, and carry yourself with pride while we are away. We will fetch you just as soon as we can..."

Seven years. At first he'd waited every day for them to return, but bit by bit, he'd given up waiting. He didn't even know what he was waiting for. It was impossible to imagine where his parents had gone, and what they were doing now. He read the letters they sent home, but they didn't tell him when his parents would come back for him. As the years went by, he'd decided they probably never would. And when he thought about it, he hoped they wouldn't. It was very hard to imagine living anywhere but in his grandmother's small village.

Thinking about his village, as he waited for his grandmother, gave Low a warm, comfortable feeling inside. He knew every person who lived there, every dog, every silly chicken. He knew the land on every side; the swamp-banked river that became wider and wider as it flowed towards the sea; the deep, mysterious forest of gigantic, creaking trees; the huge stretches of cultivated land on which the villagers grew their rice and pineapples and coconuts.

It was quite impossible for him to leave, anyhow. Who would look after Ting-Ting? Most people in the village kept pigs, and it was Low's job to look after his grandmother's sow. Each morning, he boiled up scraps for her feed and cleaned her sty. He loved grooming her with a stiff brush; she'd lie perfectly still for him while he scraped mud from her pink back. When he'd finished, he'd set out along the dusty road to school. Those who were old enough cycled the ten miles to High School. Low and his friends walked south until they got to the primary school. Low was in the top year now. Soon he'd move schools, which meant his grandmother would buy him a new uniform, new books and, with any luck, a new bike.

Low couldn't wait for that new bike. He was also looking forward to being a High School student. And before that, to the birth of Ting-Ting's piglets and the April holiday. Nowhere on his list of things to hope for was there a journey to a foreign land.

It took only a moment for Ee Tsang to compose herself. She rose, passed the fortune-teller his fee and shuffled off in search of candles and prayer-papers, for now she had an important petition for the Enlightened One.

I should go with her, Low thought, make her tell me what it all means. As if I can't guess.

But voices were floating in through the open temple portal. "The dragon is coming! The dragon is coming!" and Low Hee ran out into the sunlight, choosing a friendly red monster against a nameless, shapeless one.

No one wanted the festivities to end. In every home special food was laid out and there were sweets in abundance for all the children. Low and his grandmother had to visit everyone in the village, just as everyone had visited them, before the Dragon Procession. It was dark by the time they reached home, and the air was filled with the fragrant smell of the frangipani trees.

Grandmother lowered herself into a chair, took

off her best silk slippers and rubbed her feet. "I'm too old to do so much walking," she complained. "But it was a wonderful New Year, wasn't it?"

Low nodded. He had a pocket stuffed with glacé fruits and sweetmeats which he was slowly chewing his way through. He was getting more and more impatient. When would Ee Tsang tell him about the fortune-teller's predictions? He watched her kneel, as she usually did at bedtime, before the shrine of Kuan Yin, the Goddess of Mercy, which stood in one corner of their wooden bungalow. She offered up a bowl of her finest egg noodles then bowed her head in contemplation.

Low knew she'd be there for some time. While her back was turned, he practised his moves. He worked first on his arm strikes and then on his leg kicks, trying to get them as smooth as possible. Flowing movements, that was the aim. He stopped quickly when his grandmother finally began to rise. She disliked his keen interest in Kung-Fu, so he didn't practise when she could see him.

Grandmother shuffled to the ornately carved bureau where she kept her private things and took out a piece of crisp blue paper.

"I've had a letter from your father," she said, handing it to him.

Low read eagerly. His father's writing was very beautiful, the Chinese characters carefully drawn. It must take him ages to write his letters, Low thought. He read the letter through a second time. Then he folded it in two.

"It's a long way to England, isn't it?" Low asked.

"Yes, I believe it is."

"My father is a wealthy man, now, isn't he?"

Ee Tsang gave a hint of a nod. "He regularly sends me money orders in his letters. Your mother and he make Chinese dishes for the English to eat."

"Do the English like Chinese food?"

"They must do. They pay great amounts of English money for them."

"Does he have a stall, like Tai Tung?"

"No, it's not a stall. It's indoors, like a restaurant. But there are no tables." Low could see that his grandmother was as puzzled by this as he was. He was used to buying food straight from open-air stalls and eating it as he walked along in the sunshine. "But your uncle Haw has a restaurant," his grandmother was reminding him. "In the same part of England. They, also, kindly send me money orders."

"I thought..." Low found his voice was failing him. His words came out in a whisper. "I wondered if they had forgotten about me." Although often he wished that they would, secretly he wanted to be remembered and loved by the parents whose faces he found it difficult to bring to mind.

"No, no, they have never forgotten," said Ee Tsang. "But it is not easy, in a new country. It was not easy for my great-grandfather, when he came from China to live here in Malaysia. He worked in the tin mines until he was too old and worn out to enjoy the money he'd earned. Your parents have worked just as hard to make a good home for Low to live in. It has taken them all this time, but now your father is coming for you, so that you can be together."

"Honourable grandmother?" Low whispered.

"Yes, my Low Hee?"

"I don't want to go to England."

"You should be with your mother and father."

"You have always been my honoured mother."

"I am what I am. Your grandmother."

"Can't I just stay here?"

His grandmother was able to draw herself up and become several inches taller when she was displeased. "Low Hee must do as his father instructs him." She used very formal speech and clipped tones to remind Low just how little choice he had. Low bowed his head. Of course he had to follow his father's wishes. Every one of his friends had fathers who expected obedient behaviour from their children and got it, without question. That was the Chinese way, he knew that. But his father wasn't here – not yet.

He looked up at Ee Tsang with the sort of expression he used when he wanted something really badly; to go swimming instead of do his chores, or to have extra pocket money because a peddler was due in the village.

"Esteemed and noble grandmother," he began, choosing his words carefully. "In your well-earned old age, you deserve to receive the devoted attentions of a loving grandson. That is why I cannot go to England. If I leave, you will have to spend your final years alone. Surely my father will understand, if you write and explain that you are unable to lose such love and respect?"

He gave his grandmother a pleading smile. Usually, this was a winning approach. He waited, confident of the outcome.

"No," said Ee Tsang.

"But Grandmother..."

"No, Low Hee!" She grew again, swelling out of her small, thin body so that she loomed over him. "Perhaps you have lived with your grandmother for too long. You have forgotten that a son should venerate and esteem his father above all others." She took him firmly by the arm and led him to the wall opposite the shrine of the Goddess of Mercy. "Look well at this picture, Low," she said, waving her hand at a bamboo frame that hung in front of them. "Learn its lesson and undertake its message."

Low looked reluctantly at the four small pictures inside the frame. They told a story of Chinese life that always made him feel very uncomfortable.

In the first scene, an old man lay asleep on his bed in the heat of the afternoon. Mosquitoes hovered all around him, biting him and disturbing his rest. In the next two pictures, the old man's son, observing the way his father tossed and turned, tried to flap the insects away, but when this failed, he removed all his clothes and stood close to the bed. In the final scene, the father was at last able to sleep in peace. Every mosquito was enjoying the smooth, bare skin of the dutiful son.

"It is my duty, I suppose," said Low, looking at the picture and shuddering, "to be with my father."

Ee Tsang gave him a wide smile. "My son would be proud to hear his son say those words." But she added, in almost a secret whisper between them, "And you mustn't worry about me. I've got many friends in this village. Someone will look after the pigs."

Low felt breathless and tight inside. When he looked down, he found he'd folded the letter from England so many times, it was now a damp and grubby square no bigger than a postage stamp.

CHAPTER TWO

"I expect your son would like the window seat, Mr Tang."

The airline stewardess was a pretty, smiling Malaysian girl. Low shuffled between the rows of seating and plonked himself down. The furnishings were comfortable, but they gave off a strange smell that made him feel queasy. The magazines his father had bought him at the Chinese bookstall were damp beneath his touch. He looked out of the window. His father settled into the next seat. Low continued to look out of the window.

"Well, Low Hee," said his father.

Low struggled to think of something to say. Some general topic which they could both nod politely over. He tore his eyes away from the scene outside. "The buildings in Kuala Lumpur are very tall, aren't they, Father?"

"You have not seen your capital city before?" His father sounded reproachful.

"No," Low shook his head. "My honourable grandmother cannot travel now. We live quietly in our village. I don't mind."

"What a country boy you are," said Father, and his mouth moved into a line that might have been interpreted as a smile, or perhaps it was a sneer.

Low sighed. He turned the pages of his

magazines, but couldn't read. Nothing, he thought, seemed to please his father. From his momentous arrival at their small bungalow, Wye Liew Tang had nagged away and picked at his son's appearance, his education, his behaviour.

"Does Low Hee not speak any English yet?" his father had asked, perplexed.

"No, Father. Next year, when I move up to secondary school."

"Your first task will be to learn English. As soon as we arrive, we shall begin instruction."

Then, moments later: "He is not very tall yet, Mother, is he?" and, "Eeeah! Look at his teeth! They have rotted away. You have spoilt him with sweetmeats!" and, "Has Low Hee attended the temple regularly? Does he know the four noble truths, the eightfold path?"

Wye Liew Tang had led Low out on to the bungalow veranda and they had settled themselves on the wooden chairs. A cloud of scarlet butterflies were flirting with the flowers his grandmother grew.

From his jacket pocket, Wye Liew produced two glossy photographs. "This is our shop," he said, showing the first one to Low. "Very soon, it will be your home." For the first time, he smiled, and Low saw a flash of gold as he displayed the fillings in his teeth. "You will have your own bedroom. Your mother has been very busy making it nice for you."

Low looked at the picture. It was taken from the street. A brick building with a large window at the front. Low pointed to the letters that were displayed above the shop-front. "English," he commented.

"It says, 'Tang's Take-Away'," said his father. He spoke the words in English and then tried to explain them in Cantonese. "People come in, order their food, we cook it, they pay for it and take it away to eat. You will be able to help us serve the customers. I want you to become part of our business."

Low nodded. He was trying to keep his mind on what his father was saying, but Koong, one of his friends, was waving furiously as he passed the bungalow on his way to his father's market garden. Low lifted his arm tentatively and wriggled his fingers at Koong.

"This is where your uncle and aunt live," his father continued, passing him the other photograph. The picture showed a grand restaurant, quite different from Tang's Take-Away. Chinese characters made from neon lights proclaimed this was 'The House of Haw'. "Your great-grandfather also lives there. He is the head of our family. He settled in England with his daughter, many years ago. This daughter had a son – your uncle Haw..."

Low's mind wandered, along with his eyes...A solitary buffalo stood in the nearest paddy field. On its back perched a white cattle egret, who was considerately picking the ticks from the buffalo's tough skin and enjoying them...

"Low! Pay attention!" His father flicked his knuckles across the back of Low's hand and the photographs fell to the floor. Low bent quickly to retrieve them. His father's words stung as they dropped down on to him. "You will have to lose these dreamy, country-boy ways in England. It's very different there."

"I liked being a country boy," he muttered to himself, furiously flicking the pages of his magazine and sinking even further down into the soft aeroplane seating. He wanted to poke his tongue out to its farthest extent at someone, he wanted to yell, he wanted to escape back to his village. Then, as the engines began to vibrate through the body of the plane, and he heard the instructions to put on his safety-belt, he wanted to be very sick.

The ground moved away from them, then the airport buildings, then the city. He looked down and saw all of Malaysia slipping from him, getting smaller and more distant every second.

He wished his grandmother could have been there, waving.

Mr Tang brought some maps out of his hand luggage and laid them on his son's lap, hiding the magazines.

"This is where we shall be landing – here, at this airport, Heathrow," he said. "This," his hand swept over most of the rest of the page, "is the largest city you will ever see. London. It has many more buildings than Kuala Lumpur. It is a shame I shall not be able to show you London when we arrive, Low Hee. You would be amazed."

"Is that where you and Mother live?"

"No. Now we have a shop in a place called Bristol. We will go straight there in my car."

"You've got a car?" asked Low, his eyes widening with delight.

"Nearly everyone in England has a car." Wye Liew's stern mouth broke into a grin. The car was his pride and joy. He turned a page of the map and traced his clean fingernail along a thick, blue line. "This is Bristol."

"Bis Toll." Low tried out the sounds. "Lon Don."

"And look, Low Hee, do you see this tiny writing here?" his father sounded very excited, so Low bent to examine the page, but all he could see was the criss-cross of coloured lines. "Here is Littlecoot, where we have our shop, Tang's Take-Away. We have lived there ever since your sister was born."

"SISTER!" Low exclaimed. "I have a sister?" He couldn't believe it. No one, not even his grandmother, who must have known, had ever breathed a word about a sister!

"Hush," his father ordered, as several heads turned towards the noise. "Please!"

"You didn't tell me!" cried Low, now almost in tears.

"She is only very little, a tiny baby."

"You should have told me," said Low, pounding the map with his fists. *Why* hadn't they told him?

Was he not part of their family?

"I *am* telling you," said his father, but he sounded uncomfortable, and didn't scold Low for his outburst, except to add, "A son of Tang does not cry out, not in pain or anger."

"It was surprise," said Low. "I was surprised, that's all." His fists pounded the map relentlessly, until his father took it away.

Low stared out of the window again, into the suffocating whiteness of the clouds. His stomach was rolling round inside him with an intensity that was impossible to ignore, and when the smiling stewardess came back to take their orders for a meal, the thought of food made Low retch so badly she whipped a paper bag under his chin and held it there, her sweet smile never faltering, while Low heaved the sour contents of his stomach into it.

CHAPTER THREE

Until his father unlocked the boot with his key and threw in their luggage, Low had doubted the existence of a family car. But here it was, red and shiny, with his father holding open a door for him. He clambered in and tried to snuggle into the seat for warmth. He felt very ill indeed, hot inside, yet shivering with cold. His father had warned him that winter weather was chilly in England, but he hadn't been expecting the bitter wind that greeted them the moment they stepped off the plane.

"How is my son's stomach, now?" asked Wye Liew Tang, as he pulled out from the car park.

Low looked down at his body, as though the offending part might speak for itself. The rush of oncoming cars that whizzed past them, and the way his father moved swiftly out into their stream, made him feel even more dizzy. He imagined replying with the sort of answer that would please a father; "Never again will a plane be my master. Next time, I will enjoy my voyage," or, "Now the sickness is over, I have a good appetite for the rest of the day."

But all he could manage, through his cold and dizziness, was a grunt. He flopped against the headrest, eyes closed. His mind swirled away from the ugly, square grey buildings they travelled between, back to the warmth of the land of his birth...

...The heat of the tropical sun washed over him. He lay back in the flat-bottomed boat they sometimes borrowed and listened to Koong, who was chattering on about what he'd done the previous weekend.

"Caves – really deep – up in hills on the other side of Crik. We had to pull ourselves along this tunnel and then suddenly we were in this massive cavern as big as a temple. I was glad I was wearing my basketball boots because there are snakes all over the floor. Dad said they only ate the bats. He shone his torch up to the roof and there they were – millions of them, all hanging upside-down. Bats!"

The two boys floated slowly through the swamps, past the mangrove trees with their long, pale roots that reached down into the water like thirsty snakes. When they came to the open river, they pulled off their T-shirts and shorts and dived in. The coolness of the water felt wonderful on their hot skin. They were hoping to dive like cormorants for fish, but mostly they just messed about, pushing each other under the surface and seeing how deep they could dive. Finally exhausted, they pulled themselves back into the bobbing boat, shrieking with laughter as it nearly capsized...

When he finally woke, as the car drew up outside Tang's Take-Away, he was amazed at how his dreams had warmed him through, until he realized that his father had switched on the hot-air heating.

Low's mother was standing outside their shop. Low had been afraid he wouldn't recognize her, but as soon as he saw the slender woman with the almond-shaped face and feathery fringe, he knew who it was.

Low suddenly came to life. He flung himself out of the car and round on to the pavement, ready for the hugs and kisses that welcoming smile promised. He didn't see the tiny child she was holding by the hand until he was nearly on top of her. Huge black eyes gazed steadily at him. Low gazed back, at the rosebud mouth, the clean white socks in black patent shoes and the red satin bow in the silky hair.

His sister was a pretty little thing, he thought, but his father hadn't been quite truthful. She was not a baby.

"You have grown so much, Low," said his mother. "I would not have believed it possible." She reached out, with her slender fingers, and was about to pull him to her, but his father put his larger hand round her tiny wrist and drew her away.

"He is not all that tall for eleven years," said Wye Liew.

"Tch!" said his mother, through her teeth. "You are mistaken, Wye. You have grown used to the English boys. No, Low is tall for his age." She smiled at Low, but didn't touch him.

"Perhaps you're right, Sau," acknowledged Wye, in a voice that suggested his son had been disappointing enough already, without the further worry of height.

"Say hello to Mui Kit," said his mother, giving the little girl a push forward.

For a moment or two, Low could not move. As he looked down at his sister, he remembered his grandmother's words: *"Your parents have worked hard to make a good home for Low to live in."* Why hadn't she mentioned a sister, already living in it? Why? And when his father showed him the photograph of Tang's Take-Away, he could have taken that opportunity to tell him. Why had no one explained? And why hadn't his parents sent Mui Kit to Malaysia, for his grandmother to look after? Why was it easy for them to keep their daughter, but not their son? They *had* forgotten him, he thought. Not completely, but enough. It was like forgetting to play with a friend who lived in another village. You kept *meaning* to walk over to see them, but you never quite managed it.

Mui Kit was staring at him with interest. She took the two fingers she'd been sucking out of her mouth and jabbed him in the chest with them, tickling him a bit. "Hel-lo," she said, in English.

Low picked up the little girl. He was used to carrying small children around his village. "Hel-lo, Mui Kit," he replied, trying to copy the way she'd said it. He gave the top of her head a peck with his lips and put her on her feet again.

As they went indoors, he realized that so far, she was the only member of his new family he had hugged or kissed.

Tang's Take-Away had three large rooms downstairs

and four smaller ones upstairs. The way in was through the shop entrance. They passed through a flap in a long counter made from planks of wood. On the counter was a till and a television. By the door a row of tall stools patiently waited for customers. The walls were lined with shelves filled with chopsticks, sweet and sour sauces in bottles, Pepsi Cola and pickled onions. Everything was painted a rich shade of coral pink.

They passed through the second room, which was the kitchen. Low hardly had time to notice the big fridge, the chest freezer and the two large hobs full of gas rings before they moved into the room beyond.

"This room is for the family," said Sau Kit, with pride in her voice. "Somewhere we can relax when we're not working in the shop." A flicker of doubt crept into her expression. "That doesn't happen very often yet," she added. "We seem to work from the moment we get up to the moment we go to bed."

"That will change, now that Low is here," said his father.

Low looked round the room. He spotted one familiar sight, a shrine in the corner. But instead of Grandmother's Goddess of Mercy, a fat, porcelain Buddha sat on the shelf, its usual gushing smile in place. There were two sofas, both very old and shabby, positioned on either side of a small gas fire. Low was drawn to the fire. He hadn't realized he'd been shivering with cold, until he sat on the edge of the sofa nearest the warmth. Even his bones felt chilled.

"I will make a tray of tea," said his mother. "To warm you up. Then tomorrow we'll go into town and buy you some new clothes. Nothing in your suitcase is suitable for the English winter. A couple of nice warm tracksuits, that's what you need."

"And some school clothes," added Wye. "He must start school as soon as possible."

"School," said Low. He had only ever been to one school. The thought of starting at a completely strange new school filled him with dread, but he hid his fears. He was pretty certain that his father would expect him to be excited, and pleased. "Is it...is it a big school?" he asked.

"I've only been inside once," Wye replied. "To discuss your admission with the headmaster. It is called Littlecoot Comprehensive. I think there are about a thousand children attending."

"A *thousand*!" echoed Low, in horror. Even the High School he'd been looking forward to was not that big.

Luckily, his father assumed that he was simply surprised. "It's not far away," he went on. "Once you know the way, you'll be able to walk there in less than half an hour."

"I expect you'll soon make lots of English friends," said Sau, coming in with a bamboo tray of tea.

"Are there any Chinese boys at the school?" asked Low.

"You'll have to find that out for yourself," said

Wye. "But the most important thing is for you to learn English. If you make friends with English children, that will help you learn."

"I know a few words," said Low, eager to please. "Yeh, noh, pliss, tan-kew, hel-lo. And Bis-tol. London."

Wye bowed his head in acknowledgement. "You will have to use the shortened form of your name when you are at school," he added. "English teachers have trouble with the superior sounds of Cantonese. For them, Low will be enough. We call your sister Kitty, now. They can say that without trouble."

"Kitty doesn't go to school, does she?" asked Low.

"Of course not, she is only three," said his mother. "She goes to a place for playing, called a playgroup."

Kitty had been sitting on her mother's knee, but when she heard her name mentioned she wriggled down and began picking up all her toys, which were scattered over the vinyl flooring. She handed them, one by one, to Low.

"Teddy," she said, her English coming easily, as she passed him an ancient bear. "Train." Soon, Low's arms were full and he'd added several new words to his vocabulary.

"Car," he repeated after her. "Rabbit."

Kitty obviously wanted to be friends. Low was still smarting from the discovery of her existence, but her smile was so wide and unassuming that he couldn't help but smile back and pretend to play with the toys.

"Kitty is teaching Low English," observed his mother, happily.

"That is good," said Wye. His stern expression softened just a bit as he watched his daughter play. "We must open the shop again tomorrow," he added, as if reminded of the fact by something. "It has been shut all the time I've been away."

"We will soon be as busy as ever," sighed Sau.

"But it will be easier with another pair of hands and feet," Wye replied quickly, looking keenly at his son.

Low's bedroom was the coldest place he had ever been in. After something to eat, his mother took him on a tour of the little house, which ended with her saying, "And this will be your bedroom, Low."

She ushered him into a tiny boxroom with an iron-framed bed and a chest of drawers. There was a small window that let in a little light and a considerable amount of cold air.

When his mother left him, telling him he should unpack his bags, the first thing he did was try to shut the window. But it stuck ajar, and the bitter winds whipped through the gap and made him shudder.

Looking out, he could see the restaurant's back yard in the light from the downstairs window. It was full, just full up with black plastic sacks. Low gazed down on them, wondering what could be inside. He imagined they were full of rice or noodles, perhaps ready for cooking.

Behind the little garden, one dim lamp illuminated a narrow lane. It was the only thing he'd seen, since landing at Heathrow, that reminded him at all of home. It was not lined with brightly coloured flowers, and the bushes were very different from the trees and shrubs of Malaysia, but the slats of the wooden sheds and fences reminded him of the way his grandmother's bungalow was constructed. He couldn't see all the lane, because the small, flat-roofed garage that took up one corner of the yard prevented him, but for ages he stared and stared out into the growing darkness until he was almost numb with cold.

His fingers were too stiff to do any unpacking. He climbed into the creaky bed and discovered he was too short for it, so that to be comfortable he had to curl up. He wound himself into a tight ball. The rough blanket scratched at his chin, but he was too exhausted to care. He closed his eyes and in seconds was asleep.

CHAPTER FOUR

"Low – do you understand me? Do...you...understand ...me?" asked Ms Berkley.

Low stared at the teacher, his mouth solemnly closed. If only he could understand what she said.

The first day at his new school had arrived only too quickly. Yesterday, his mother had taken him to buy his new clothes. His father had already started work in the kitchen when they left, cleaning surfaces and preparing raw ingredients.

"Try to be back for opening time," he told Sau.

"What time does the shop open?" Low asked as he'd waited for Kitty to be buckled into her car seat.

"Twelve o'clock," she replied. "We shall have to be swift."

Low was used to shopping in a leisurely fashion. When his grandmother went marketing, she walked slowly from stall to stall and stood for ages, inspecting the goods displayed. She'd bargain with the stall holder until she was sure she'd been offered a fair price, carefully check her change and stow her goods neatly in her basket. After she'd purchased everything she'd come for, she'd join her friends and drink bowls of scalding tea while Low and Koong played hide and seek round the stalls.

His mother had a different way of
They dropped Kitty off at her playgroup at half past

nine and drove to a multi-storey car park near the shopping centre. Then they hurried from shop to shop, ticking off the things Sau Kit had written down on her list as they made their purchases.

"School bag," Sau muttered. She hurried Low into a store which was full of bags of all sizes and shapes and said, "Ah, this one, I think," plonking a backpack on the counter. By eleven o'clock, Low had carrier bags heavy with a complete set of school uniform, a tracksuit, some jeans and warm sweatshirts, a cosy pair of pyjamas, an outdoor jacket and a new pair of lace-up shoes.

By the time they picked up Kitty from playgroup, Low's head was buzzing. He'd always thought his grandmother's marketing was boring, but now he longed to be standing by her side as she haggled for hours over a length of silk.

When they arrived back, Sau tied a white apron round her trim waist and scurried into the shop.

Low flopped down on to a sofa. A spring bounced back at him in protest. Kitty wanted to show him the soggy painting she'd brought home with her. "Very nice," he agreed, trying to keep the paint off his clothes. "I start school tomorrow," he'd told her. "I bet I don't bring back a picture of a teddy."

And now, here he was, in the third lesson of the first morning. He was sitting between a boy and a girl who were chatting in half whispers across the table in their flat, bewildering language. His head buzzed with the foreign words. His father had recommended that he repeat out loud every word spoken to him in English, but he'd already given up doing that. After the first few times, the rest of the class had fallen off their chairs with mirth and someone had set up a chant at the back of the room, something that sounded like, "Pah-rot, pah-rot".

Low spent most of his time gazing round the room, hopeful of spotting at least one other Chinese amongst the thirty bobbing heads, but the class was a sea of squashy pink faces above white shirts and navy jumpers, topped with brownish lumps of hair.

He searched for anything that might distinguish a person, and his gaze settled on a girl sitting at a table near the front. Her hair was as black as his, and hung in a long ponytail down her back. He recognized her as being Asian, probably Indian, immediately. She saw him scrutinising her and smiled at him. He turned his gaze modestly away, and did not look her way again.

"Low," said Ms Berkley, coming right up to him. "Can you understand me?"

Low chose the safest reply. "Noh."

"Be quiet!" yelled the teacher at the rest of the class. She sighed. "What were we going to do today?"

"Climate, Miss!" a handful of pupils returned.

"Climate, Miss," sang out one fox-faced boy at the back. "Spelt B-O-R-I-N-G, Miss! Oops, sorry, I mean Ms. Sounds like Mzzz." And in a loud whisper to the boy next to him, "Ms means the same as Miss but older, see?"

"I think we'll veer from the syllabus just for this morning," said Ms Berkley, taking a deep breath. "We have a valuable source of information sitting in our midst, and we shouldn't lose the chance to use it."

"Do you mean Low, Miss?" some of the boys called. "But he can't speak any English, Miss!"

"Quite." The teacher took Low by the hand and motioned for him to follow her. At the back of the humanities room was a large map of the world. "There are some things that need no language. Music, for instance. And maps. Maps look pretty much the same all over the world." She placed a fingertip on a green blob at the top of the map. "We – are – here," she said to Low. "Britain. England."

But Low had put his finger on an island in the South China Sea. "Malaysia," he said, in imperfect tones.

"Annell, I want you to slip along to the library and get as many books on Malaysia as you can find. Get some on China, too. Ones with pictures in." Ms Berkley turned to the class.

"Malaysia is called the melting-pot of the world," she said. "Hundreds of years ago it was almost all jungle, hundreds of square miles of rain forest with a few peaceful tribal people living close to nature. But then came others from lands all around, hoping to make a fortune from the riches to be found on the island. In the last century, thousands of men and boys emigrated from China to become tin miners, and people from India and Sri Lanka came to work on the rubber plantations. Now, Malays, Indians, Chinese, Europeans and many other races all work and live side by side."

Annell returned with a pile of books. She plonked them on Ms Berkley's desk. Low was allowed to turn the pages, while the rest of the class crowded round. At first all he could say was; "Chinese – Chinese!" This was an English word he had long known. But as the pages turned, Ms Berkley would point to things and name them. "Tin mine," she said. "Paddy field. Jungle. Rubber trees. Look – a flying snake! Temple. Buddha."

"Buddha, Buddha," Low repeated. He repeated all the words, and nobody laughed now.

When the bell rang, Low was almost disappointed that the lesson had come to an end.

"Dinner bell, mate," said a boy. Low looked up to discover the boy who'd made so much noise at the back of the class, earlier on. His foxy nose and sharp teeth reminded him of the packs of stray dogs that sniffed round his grandmother's village. "Don't worry, Miss," said the boy. "I'll make sure he gets to the canteen all right."

Ms Berkley pursed her lips. "I didn't realize you had such an altruistic nature, Skiff."

"Don't be dirty, Miss," quipped Skiff, giving the teacher a wink as he ushered Low out of the classroom.

"Right, then. YOU-WANT-FOOD?" Skiff yelled into Low's ear. He made eating gestures to reinforce his point.

Low nodded. He'd been too wound up to eat breakfast, but now his appetite was returning.

"Got any money?" Skiff dug in his pocket and pulled out a sample pound coin. "DOSH, DOUGH, DOLLARS?"

"Ah!" said Low. "Dollar!" He had been given similar coins by his father before they'd left the house. He gave one to Skiff.

"You'll cough up more than that," said Skiff, jingling his pockets. "MORE DOLLAR?"

As soon as Skiff was in possession of Low's three pounds, he began to push Low roughly in the direction of the canteen. They made their way along the line of hungry pupils. Skiff bought a dinner and pudding for himself and a plate of chips and a bowl of rice pudding for Low. Swiftly, he pocketed the change from the three pounds.

Skiff hurried off to join his mates. Low followed him and grabbed the last chair at his table. He wasn't going to let the chance of making friends slip by.

"New boy," Skiff remarked to the other boys. "Chinese, Chinese." He made his voice sound like Low's had, when he'd looked in the geography books. The others began giggling. "Chinese Take-Away," said Skiff, tucking into his fried fish. "We're going to have a lot of fun with Chinese Take-Away, I reckon. A *lot* of fun." He pointed to the bowl of rice pudding. "Fond of rice, is Take-Away. Go on – eat up!"

Low took a mouthful of the pudding. It was quite obviously rice, but what a strange way of cooking it!

"Rise," Low said, practising.

The rest of the table laughed openly at him. "Stupid!" roared Skiff. "Stupid Take-Away! You're supposed to eat the chips first!"

Low's hunger drained away with the boys' laughter. He looked for chopsticks, but could see none. "Tip firs," he repeated, and picked one up in his fingers.

"Can't you use a knife and fork?" Skiff almost screamed at him, in delight. "Chinese Take-Away savage!"

Low had no idea what Skiff was saying, but he knew instinctively that he had not fallen among friends. He dropped the chip, and scraped back his chair.

"*Lubsup!*" he threw back at them, gesturing to his tray. Yes, he thought, English food was complete rubbish. He stormed through the randomly placed tables, stumbling once on a chair leg, and finally was out of the canteen. He lurched along the corridors until he was in the fresh air and lowered himself on to some stone steps.

A fine drizzle was coming down. Low stayed on the steps until his hair and jumper were drenched and he was shivering with the cold. After what seemed a long time, he decided to go to the room they had started in that morning. But when he went back in, he realized he had no idea where he was. This school building was far bigger than his Chinese primary school in the Malay countryside. He was totally lost in it.

He wandered along the corridors, peering into each classroom as he passed for anything he might recognize. At first, the place was deserted, but as he walked on and on it began to fill up again with crowds of foreign faces, the ubiquitous pinkness occasionally relieved by brown or black. They all strode past him with infuriating nonchalance and vitality.

Then a bell rang out, and everyone began to speed up, become more purposeful. Low panicked. He looked wildly around. It was obvious the dinner-hour was over, but he had no idea where to meet his class.

"Low!"

He spun round at the sound of his own name and came face to face with the girl with the long black ponytail.

"Are you lost?" She grabbed his arm and took him with her, swinging her bag on to the other shoulder. "Look, my name's Henna, right?" She stopped, and did a little mime in the middle of the corridor. "You...Low. Me...Henna," and then giggled.

Low broke out into smiles at such simple clarity.

"Understand?" asked the girl, smiling back.

"Yeh," said Low, nodding furiously. They

grinned at each other, both enjoying their achievement.

"So let's swing through this jungle, right?" giggled Henna, opening the door to the tutor room. "Didn't they give you anyone to look after you on your first day? Miserable lot. Never mind, Low, you stick with me. I'll see you're OK. I won't let the jungle get to you."

CHAPTER FIVE

"First, cash-and-carry," said Wye Liew Tang, as Low climbed wearily into the car after school.

"What is that?" he asked. His father had spoken the words in English.

"A sort of warehouse, very useful. You will see."

They drove out of town. Low, expecting his father to ask him about his first day at school, began practising his replies. He didn't want to say anything that might sound like moaning, but how was he to avoid that, and tell the truth? He looked out of the window in despair.

Mr Tang swung the car into a large car park. As he pulled on the hand brake, he cast a surreptitious glance at his son. He had been expecting Low to tell him about his first day at school, and to ask questions about the cash-and-carry, but Low did not appear to like talking, unlike his sister, who chattered on from the time she got up to the time she went to bed.

Wye Liew was not at all used to boys, he admitted to himself. He could hardly remember what it had been like to be eleven. But surely *he* hadn't shown so little interest in *his* father's business affairs? Low was staring ahead, out of the window. When Wye Liew looked more closely at the serious countenance, he was sure that his son was sulking.

He let out a sigh. He'd looked forward to Low coming to England so much. He'd imagined a boy with energy and enthusiasm, who'd be keen to help build up the take-away, who'd share his dream of one day buying a restaurant like his cousin Haw owned. He wanted to tell Low about his dream, and the hard work they'd all have to put in if it was to be realized, but it was difficult to talk intimately with someone who stared away from you all the time.

He took one of the large trolleys and pushed it into the cash-and-carry. He went up and down the aisles, dragging down the heavy cardboard boxes from tall piles and balancing them on the trolley. He looked back at Low, who was keeping behind him.

"Are you paying attention to what we are doing here?" he asked. His voice snapped with the anger that was building up inside him. He took a deep breath to control it. He could not lose his temper in this public place.

Low heard the angry snap in the words. His father had not spoken to him during the whole of the journey, except to say where they were heading, and now, suddenly, he was cross with him. At first, he'd been relieved that his father had avoided the subject of school, but bit by bit he began to feel very sour.

"Well, if he's not interested in me, I'm not going to be interested in his stupid cash-and-carry," he told himself. But it wouldn't have been dutiful to say such a thing. He hung his head and mumbled an apology he didn't feel.

"We are shopping for stock," said Wye, turning again to his trolley. "When we run low on potatoes, fish or meat, they are delivered, but cans and bottles and packets we come here and buy in bulk. That saves us money. More profit for us, do you see?"

Quickly, Low nodded. Was his father interested in nothing but making money? In his grandmother's village nobody cared about profits. If they had a bad season, they ate frugally. If they had a good season, they ate well. It was simple.

"I write out a list as we run out of stock – you see I am carrying it now – and then I come here. It is important to load the trolley carefully, so that things do not get squashed at the bottom, or fall off the top. Now, this is something we use a lot, so I will buy..."

Low stared around him. The warehouse was a high building, and Low could see the metal girders inside the roof. Small, brown birds flew and fluttered around, perching on the high girders. Everything in England is a boring brown colour, Low thought, even the birds.

"Are you attending, boy?" His father had pushed the trolley to the back of a queue of people and was searching in his pockets for his wallet.

"Father, how do the birds get in here?"

Mr Tang's face darkened with impatience. "How am I to know? Through small holes in the rafters, I suppose. Have you been listening to what I've been saying about credit cards?"

It was nearly opening time when they got home. His mother was already at work. Mr Tang carried in the first box, puffing under the weight of catering-sized baked beans. Low followed with a pack of dried mushrooms. The aromas that wafted from a wok simmering on the hob filled his whole being with hunger.

"Did you have a good day, son?" asked Sau, with her usual smile. She was chipping peeled potatoes by passing them though a hand-operated chipper. A plastic bucket full of them stood by her feet.

"Tip," said Low, pointing.

"You have learnt some English, at any rate," said Mr Tang, grudgingly. He hadn't yet forgiven Low for his sulks at the cash-and-carry.

"But did you have a good day?" persisted Sau.

"You don't go to school for fun," his father pointed out. "It will be hard at first. That is without doubt."

"Was it hard, son?"

Low shrugged. "In my old school, I was one of the eldest children," he said. "Now, I am one of the youngest." He'd decided in the car that this was a fairly safe complaint.

"You will get used to it," said his father. "Now, you must help."

"Ah yes!" cried Low, delighted. "What can I prepare for you, Father? Grandmother taught me how to use a wok when I first went to school. And I can use a sharp knife, safely. I could slice the

...getables. Or even wash things up..." he added, looking at his father's impassive stare.

"You can keep Kitty from getting under our feet," came the disappointing reply.

"Mother, when do we eat?" asked Low. Yesterday, they had all eaten together during the time the shop was closed, between half-past two and five o'clock. They'd had some supper when the shop closed at twelve midnight, then finally, his parents had sent him off to bed. Low had been so exhausted this morning after such a late night that he was sure he couldn't wait up for supper again.

"Are you hungry, son?"

"Starving."

"Did you spend the money I gave you on a meal?" asked his father.

"Yes, all of it, but—"

"Then you can't be very hungry."

"I will bring you something as soon as there is time," said Sau. "At six or seven o'clock."

Low went into the back room and flopped on to a sofa. His stomach growled constantly. The delicious smells from the kitchen didn't help. It would be impossible to wait until six or seven o'clock.

At exactly five o'clock, Sau unlocked the door to the shop and customers began to trickle in. She and Wye Liew flew about, from counter to cooker, from cooker to storeroom.

Low peeped out into the kitchen. There were

times when both his parents were not there. He crept towards the hobs. Saliva worked around his mouth. He stuffed several pieces of thinly sliced pork that were sizzling in a wok into his mouth. They were only half cooked, and burnt his mouth, but—

"EEEAH! Low!"

His father was behind him, spinning him round. He tried to swallow the meat, but he had not chewed it well enough to get rid of it quickly.

"Thief!" His father raised his hand and brought it down across the side of Low's face. Low half fell from the blow. He covered his face with his hands in self-defence.

"Spit it out!" His father stood over him, his hands on his hips. Low let the delicious morsels drop into his cupped palms. Wye Liew pointed to the rubbish bin and Low dropped the meat into it. "Customer first," said his father. "Family after. Go to your bed. Wake up tomorrow an honest boy. Not a thief."

"I didn't—" began Low.

"Go!" thundered his father.

Low threw himself out of the kitchen and yanked the door shut. He picked up one of Kitty's plastic toys and flung it at the wall. Then he belted up the stairs and into his bedroom. He dived into his bed, hiding entirely under the blankets. But after a while he climbed out of bed, too hungry and angry to fall asleep.

e leant against the ice-cold window and looked down into the back lane. In the dim light he could almost believe that, if he stepped out into it, he would be in the lanes around his village.

It was then that he saw the Chinese boy, standing half in shadow, a boy in a dark jacket and small, flat-topped hat. His round face was staring, straight up at Low's window.

"They never said," he whispered to himself. "They never told me there was another Chinese family round here."

He tapped on the window pane and gave a slight wave. The boy did not move. Low tapped harder. Still there was no response. Low opened the window fully, gasping slightly as the cold air rushed at him, and called down. "Ho!"

The boy had gone. He must have slipped back into his own garden while Low was fiddling with the window catch. Now he wished he hadn't bothered. It was probably a trick of the dim lamplight that had made it seem as if the boy had been looking up.

Bitterly cold, Low got back under the blankets fully clothed.

Sometime, he thought, I must find out where that boy lives. He rolled on to his side and breathed in the warm, hairy smell of the blankets.

Into the darkness of the tent they formed came pictures of his Malaysian village. The way he used to run into the forest and play in the green shade of the gigantic trees. It was the greenness he missed the most in this grey, English winter. In Malaysia it was always sunny, but there were warm breezes that cooled hot skin. A drying wind, his grandmother called them. Sometimes, she'd take her washing to a place where the river ran clear and shallow over rocks and rub the clothes against the stones as the water ran fast over them, and sing, sing...

This singing filled his head, and his body relaxed. The darkness swirled, the singing welled up from inside him. Then, distantly at first, he saw the face he'd seen from the window. He was nearly asleep, his breathing regular and deep, when the Chinese boy's face swam into perspective. It was as pale and smiling as a full moon and surrounded by the music, his grandmother's high voice...

BANG!

Low's eyes flew open. He had been high up somewhere, asleep and dreaming, and suddenly he'd dropped from that height and was awake. He'd had weird dreams like this before, waking with a bang after falling through space. His heart thumped fast and strong below his ribs. He pushed back the blankets. He was sticky with sweat. He had an odd, tantalizing feeling in the pit of his stomach, as if he should be able to recall something wonderful, if only he could scrape the memories together.

"What did I dream?" he asked himself. But as he racked his brain for the elusive image, his eyes closed and he fell properly asleep.

CHAPTER SIX

"Open wide," said the dentist.

He smiled at Low. Low smiled back. He was delighted. He'd understood the words. They meant something to him.

"Open wide," the dentist repeated. He leant over the prostrate Low, a fine steel probe between his fingers.

Low struggled to sit up. "I do not understand you," he gabbled in rapid Cantonese. "I speak absolutely no English."

The dentist continued to smile. His outward good humour didn't fool Low. He had heard of dentists; friends from his old school had told tales of dentists. He'd been lucky – he had a grandmother who understood a boy's terror – lucky until now, at least.

"Grandmother," he whimpered, under his breath, hating himself for his lack of courage. He gritted his teeth together.

"I think," said the dentist. "We might get on faster if Mr Tang – your father – was in here with you. He could translate."

Almost instantly, Low's mouth shot open. It was as if the dentist had flicked a switch. The fine steel probe floated before Low's eyes. It hovered over the gaping hole his lips had formed before plunging from view. He could feel it, prodding about by his gums.

"Just call Mr Tang," said the dentist to his nurse, when he was done.

Low flashed him a hurt look. He felt cheated. He had opened his mouth for this man on the silent promise that his father would stay outside.

"Ah," said the dentist, as Low's father came in. "Your son has a considerable amount of dental decay, Mr Tang. Some of the back teeth will have to come out, I'm sorry to say. Most of them will need filling. I'm keen to start today. Just a couple of fillings near the front, before more damage takes place."

"Yes, yes," agreed Mr Tang. "Please, go ahead. We want the very best for our son."

"Could you explain to Low for me?" asked the dentist, drawing up a syringe of local anaesthetic.

Mr Tang turned to Low. "The dentist is going to fill two of your teeth. He will give you an injection to prevent any pain. Be brave, my son."

Why should I need to be brave, Low wondered, if it's not going to hurt?

He closed his eyes tightly, to correspond to the way his lips stretched open. My father is a liar, he thought, as the needle slid on its stinging route, and my schoolmates were not exaggerating.

His father drove him straight to school.

"You must not eat for two hours," he told Low.

"But it is now only ten o'clock. It should not affect your lunch."

"Dinner's at half-past twelve," said Low. His father handed him three more pound coins. He shoved them deep into a trouser pocket.

"I will be at the school early this afternoon," his father called to him as Low walked away from the car. "I have an appointment with your headmaster at two-thirty."

Low came back. "What...can I ask my father what it is about?" His dead tongue fumbled for the right words.

"It is impossible to teach someone who cannot speak the language of the class, your teacher says," said Mr Tang. "I think the headmaster wishes to recommend you are put in some sort of special group."

Low's hands clenched into tight lumps of iron. He knew about special classes, but he also knew he was not slow to learn. He had only just started to get used to the class he was in. He didn't want to move into a special class. He knew he was good at most school subjects, when he learnt them in his own language.

"I do not need such help," he said. "Please tell the headmaster. I will learn English quickly. I can already understand bits."

Wye Liew bowed his head slightly. He was impressed with Low's answer, and the way he hadn't cried out in the dentist's chair, but he said nothing.

He didn't want the boy to become conceited.

I won't move away from this class, thought Low, as his father drove off. I couldn't bear to walk into another new classroom, with another set of strange faces. I shall have to try even harder.

But he knew, as the morning progressed and he trailed with his class from room to room, that the lessons were making little sense to him. His chin and his fists tightened as he struggled to understand what was going on.

I'm not learning anything, he thought, although this was quite untrue. Low *was* learning, the new words and ideas that floated around him were soaked up, absorbed without him realizing it.

He noticed that no teacher gave him a textbook of his own, as if they all expected him to be leaving the class soon. Henna was always the first to offer to share with him, but although he was grateful for her support, it meant that he found himself sitting on a table full of girls, away from the boys he longed to make friends with.

When the bell for dinner sounded, Henna was nowhere to be seen. She had gone out halfway through the last lesson and had not come back. He was swept along as the class rushed as a body to the door. He found himself in the centre of a group of boys. He recognized Skiff.

"Al'right then?" said Skiff. "You hungry, Chinese Take-Away?"

"Chinese take-way?" repeated Low, recognizing

the words. He rubbed the side of his mouth, which had felt tingly and painful all morning. The discomfort had got him down, a final niggling torment in a world of torments.

Skiff laughed, punching his mates on their arms to encourage their laughter. "See? He knows his name already."

"Leave him alone," said one of Skiff's band.

"Leave *me* alone Glyn," Skiff snapped back. "Or else, right?"

"Don't mean no harm, do you, Skiff?" said another.

"That's right, Al. No harm. Got any dollar, today, Take-Away?"

"Noh." Low's fist closed over his three pound coins. "Noh dollar."

"Oh yeah? How you gonna feed your face then?"

"Noh dollar."

"Come on, hand it over. I'll see you get fed."

"Noh."

Skiff exchanged silent glances with the other boys. "Outside," he said, and the pace and course of the group changed. Low found he was being carried along in the middle of them until they were in the yard.

"C'mon, lads, let's frisk him!" Skiff began to pat Low down his sides, slapping with the flats of his hands.

Low batted Skiff's hands away from him with his

own fists. He didn't want to start a fight. He didn't want to get in trouble on the day his father was due in the headmaster's office. Besides, he couldn't forget that his grandmother disapproved of boys fighting, even in fun, and this wasn't fun.

Skiff caught Low's hands, holding them by the wrists in a tight grip. "Want to make it harder?" he hissed, his mouth close to Low's. "Al'right, if that's how you like it..." They were struggling now, Low trying to free himself, Skiff hanging on grimly. We're a match for each other, Low thought. When he'd wrestled with friends, it was always the first thing he tried to assess. Which of them was the stronger. Skiff and he were very even, and it soon became obvious that Skiff thought so, too. "Hold him for me, will ya?" he yelled at the other boys. Suddenly, Low found Al and Glyn hanging firmly on to his wrists.

"Right, Take-Away," Skiff sneered. "You are for it." He dug his hands deep into Low's trouser pockets, and the coins at the bottom made a low chinking sound as his fingers touched them.

A fierce pain ripped across Skiff's chin and he flew over the yard, landing on his back on the cold concrete. In the same moment, Low brought his arms rapidly up and down again, forcing the other two boys to release their grip. Low took a step back, and without even thinking, assumed the position of attack: feet apart but balanced, fingers stiff and straight, ready to chop. His eyes blazed, his expression dark and alien.

"What happened?" groaned Skiff, still on his knees.

Al and Glyn were backing away. "He kicked you," said Al. "You know – Kung Foo – Haya! Haya!" He gave a half-hearted impression.

"No dollar," growled Low. He allowed himself a quick look round. Had he been seen? But Skiff hadn't wanted an audience any more than Low did, and he'd chosen a place not overlooked by any windows.

"C'mon," said Skiff, glancing warily at Low. He prodded at his jaw as he got to his feet. "Let Take-Away find his own way to the canteen, seeing he's so flamin' smart."

The boys disappeared through the doors and scooted off down the corridor.

But Low had wandered the building enough times now to be getting a gist of its layout, and in any case he was able to follow the aroma of cooking to the canteen with no problem. As he pushed through the swing doors, Henna ran to catch him up, tucking her arm through his.

"You made it! I was a bit worried you'd get lost without me... My oboe lesson finished late, Miss Hicks is a bit like that, anyways let's go and get some eats."

"Eats?" repeated Low.

"You know – food, fodder, school dinner."

"Ah!" said Low. "Din-ner EEUCK..." He made

a face.

Henna laughed. "Dead right there, but I'm a vegetarian, and sometimes that's not so bad. Why don't you try it?" She banged a couple of trays down and began to help herself. "Cheese and leek pie, not too awful, and rice salad – you might like that."

They sat together, as far away from Skiff's mob as they could get. Henna showed him how to scoop rice and prong the pie with his fork. "S'easy, see? Much easier than chopsticks. Never did get the hang of them." She mimicked the action of chopsticks, grinning her warm grin.

"Low...ah...Henna." He mimed chopsticks in return.

"You teach me how to use them?"

"Yeh...Teash...Henna."

"I'm gonna turn up one night at your shop," said Henna, "and buy you right out of sweet and sour king prawn. That's my favourite, sweet'n'sour, OK?"

"Sweet'n'sour, 'kay?" said Low. He scooped up more rice salad. For a moment or two he felt less alone, less unhappy. Then he remembered the appointment his father had that afternoon and the peace that had settled on him dissolved into nothing.

CHAPTER SEVEN

"Low, bring that bucket of chips over here."

"Low, Kitty is crying, see what's wrong."

"Low, wash up these utensils."

"Low, make Kitty a drink."

"Low, empty the rubbish bins."

Low struggled with the plastic bin liners, tipping them into one big black sack. Everything slipped about, and potato peelings fell to the floor.

"Low, you are not being very careful," said his mother. She was dipping a pile of white fish into thick batter, her hands moving swiftly and elegantly as she worked. Low thought that his mother's hands never seemed to stop working. She turned and gave him a smile. "Perhaps you are not used to being given jobs?"

"At home—" Low began. He stopped himself and started again. "At my grandmother's house, I looked after Ting-Ting."

"Who is that?" asked his mother, her brow wrinkling into a dainty frown.

"Grandmother's sow."

His father suddenly burst into a laugh. Not actually *laughter*, Low thought, but even a single squawk of amusement was better than the usual scowl. "I'd forgotten about the pigs," he said, shaking his head. "We've been here so long, Sau, I'm forgetting what life in Malaysia was like. Those wretched sows! Ate everything, then furrowed as few piglets as possible."

"You're right," said Sau. "We are forgetting. We should ask Low to remind us of things."

"I could tell you about the New Year festival," said Low, eagerly.

"Later on," said his father. "We are far too busy at the moment."

"When things slow down this evening, we'll sit and take tea and listen to Low's stories," said his mother. She seemed to be looking forward to the break already.

"Mother," asked Low. "When shall I do my homework?"

"Eeeah!" cried his father. "The boy is never satisfied. Yesterday he wanted to help in the shop. Now we have found him work, he wants to do something else."

"I don't mind helping," said Low. "Only the homework from the new teacher..."

Late in the school afternoon, the headmaster's secretary had come for Low. She had swept him down the corridors, her heels clipping on the flooring, making the sound of Malaysian drums.

Low knew his father would be with the headmaster. As he entered the office, they both smiled at him. Wye Liew rarely smiled, and Low supposed that the slight movement of lips was for Mr Trenchard's sake, rather than his own.

"Low," said his father, translating Mr Trenchard's words, "your headmaster and I have decided that you need time to concentrate on learning the new language before you pursue your studies further. So you will have to move to a special unit."

"Can you ask him," said Low, in anguish, "if I'll go back to the same one afterwards?"

His father gave him a sour look. "What do you mean by *him*?" he half spat in Cantonese.

"I mean Mr Trenchard," mumbled Low.

He looked down at his still shiny leather lace-ups while the two adults spoke in English. He had soon noticed that he was the only boy in the class who wore school shoes. Everyone else sported trainers, just as they had in his village, when they'd worn anything on their feet at all. He meant to have a go at his mother about getting a pair...

"The headmaster tells me that it may be a year before your maths, as well as your English, will be up to the right standard. He says it will depend on how you progress. He thinks it unlikely you will return to the mainstream classes before September. Then you will return as a year eight pupil, all being well."

Low bowed his head slightly in acknowledgement. All being well, he thought. All being well. What did that mean? What was "well"? Suddenly he saw how little he cared about anything that was happening to him. All would be well, thought Low, if I could go home. That would be well. That would be...happiness.

The headmaster had taken them both to see the Unit. The teacher, a smiling young woman, had welcomed them in. The other kids had grinned, stopping in their work to stare at the new boy with the shiny mop of black hair. Low glared resolutely back, hating them all. Miss Hale gave Low several textbooks and some clean new exercise books and told him to go home early for the weekend, and have a look through some of the maths before he came back on Monday. Wye Liew translated. Low tucked the books into his bag and slung it over his shoulder, surreptitiously glancing at his watch. It was ten-to three and he was going home.

Perhaps Miss Hale would turn out to be OK, Low thought, as he stuffed the last of the potato peelings into the sack, tied the top, heaved it on to his shoulder, and took it into the back yard behind the take-away, throwing it on to the other sacks. It was cool in the yard, and this was pleasant after the heat of the kitchen. He stood for a while, looking round.

The yard was bordered on each of its three sides by a two-metre-high fence, except where the garage walls jutted out into the yard.

Low walked to the far end. Although too high to see over, the fencing was old and loose with plenty of good footholds. He gripped the top and pulled himself up. A sharp pain shot through his left hand, as though he'd been pierced by a large thorn. He held on with his other hand and scrabbled up until his eyes were on a level with the top.

Running along the lip of the fence was a single strand of barbed wire, which he hadn't noticed in the darkness. Low's fingers had come down on to the wire and the barbs had dug deeply into his flesh. Now he could see that the wire was looped loosely, being only stapled down every forty centimetres or so. He could easily avoid it.

He found the next foothold, pushed up a little further and leant against the fence, looking out into the lane.

The dim street lamp sent an eerie orange light over the dark greens of the bushes. Nothing moved. Low began to hum. The old song, learnt from his grandmother, gave him a bittersweet sensation of having lost something he had loved.

On the other side of the lane, leaves rustled. Low stopped his humming. He tried to make his eyes see in the dim light. Into the orange glow of the lamp came a pale, shining roundness. It was a face, topped with black hair half hidden by a flat cap.

Low knew at once that this was the same face he'd seen from his window, only now that he could see the boy more clearly he could make out his features. He stared steadfastly, afraid the boy would slip away again if he took his eyes from his face.

"Greetings." Low spoke in Cantonese without thinking, but his breath caught in his throat when the boy replied in the same language.

"Greetings." The lips parted in a smile. Teeth glinted in the lamplight. The accent was sharp and strange.

"Where do you live?" asked Low, breathing again.

The boy seemed confused for a moment. He looked about him as though he had not been in the lane before.

"Do you live in that house?" said Low, pointing to the dark roof directly behind the boy.

The boy continued to gaze around him. He shot a rather wild glance at Low. "No...I..."

"Low Hee!"

Mr Tang took the path to the fence in four strides. He snatched roughly at Low's ankle, pulling him down. "You left the back door open! I found Kitty outside, playing in the rubbish sacks. I find you, down here, not at your tasks. Lazy, thoughtless, disobedient boy!"

He raised his hand to strike Low, as he had the night before. But Low was ready this time. He struggled free of his father and ran towards the house.

Wye Liew caught up with him as he reached the door, his face full of menace and hostility. "Son of Tang should never run away from punishment," he growled. His hand reached slowly towards a thin piece of bamboo that had been thrown out into the yard. He brought it down twice, hard, across his

son's back. It fell from his hand with a light clatter.
The two looked at each other.

"I didn't think, about Kitty..." Low began.

"No. You did not think. Now go. Go to your
room. Again, no supper."

Low collected his school bag from the back
room. He stared malevolently at his sister, now
quietly chewing a grubby pink rabbit. From the
little alcove, the fat Buddha grinned his serene smile.

Low didn't remember the Chinese boy again
until he reached his room. He looked down from
his window. The lane was deserted.

He flopped down on the bed, sucking the blood
from his torn finger. He wouldn't be telling his
parents about the New Year celebrations tonight.
He was surprisingly disappointed. Since coming to
England, he'd really had no one to chat to. The
people at school didn't understand him, his parents
were always too busy and Kitty was too young.

He reached down and pulled a book from his
bag. He traced the strange lettering on the cover
with his finger. He knew what it said, anyway.
MATHEMATICS.

He opened it at the first page. Numbers were a
language he could understand. In his other school,
maths had been his favourite subject. In his other
school...

In his other school lizards peered from their
frozen stance, halfway up the wall. In the yard, the
older boys ignored the new climbing equipment,

considering it only good for the little ones. They played football or held carpenter-beetle races. After school, Low's gang would make for the river, if they could. The unlucky boys who had chores waiting for them at home would yell: "Don't let the crocodiles get you!" It helped them feel better about missing out. "Don't step on a scorpion, on your way home!" Low would yell back. Low was never needed at home after school. His free time was always his own.

"Grandmother," he whispered, as he crouched on his bed, hating himself for his weakness. A boy of nearly twelve shouldn't need to call for his grandmother. But surely Grandmother would never have let her darling Low come to England if she had known what it was like? Horribly cold and dark, with schools full of bullies. A sunless land of brick, and a language full of unpronounceable sounds. Would Grandmother have let Low go with his father if she'd known how he was made of stone, as hard and unfeeling as a temple Buddha?

"Grandmother?" he whispered again and in the thick silence of his tiny room her answers came fast.

"Yes, of course I would have let you go, *made* you go, for a boy belongs with his father and mother, should esteem and obey them. So try harder, my Low, observe your filial duties, for if you do not..."

What if I do not? Low thought, sharply – what would happen if I wasn't obedient? Would they send me back? If they thought I was no good? Back to

Grandmother? It seemed almost impossible to please his father, anyway, however hard he tried. So he suddenly wondered, why he was trying at all?

With a slow, methodic movement, Low took the first page of his maths book and ripped it out. He crumpled the paper in a tight palm before letting it fall to the floor.

"Send me back, then," he spat out into the dusty gloom. "See if I care. No one wants me in this rotten place; why should I want to be here? Send me back then. See if I care."

His resolution to learn English quickly and get out of the Unit was forgotten. One by one, he tore the pages from his maths book, tore and crumpled, tore and crumpled.

CHAPTER EIGHT

"Today we are going to 'The House of Haw'," said Sau Kit.

They were in the little lane behind the shop. Wye Liew was bringing the car out of the garage. Low stood by his mother, while Kitty ran up and down the lane until her cheeks glowed.

"Your uncle and aunt are looking forward to meeting you," said his mother. "And I am looking forward to a nice rest," she added, more quietly.

"They will want to hear about Malaysia, son," said Mr Tang, as he worked the thin layer of frost off the windscreen.

"Uh-huh," shrugged Low. The thought of the ripped maths book, which now lay in the bottom of his school bag, made his tongue thick with terror, as if he'd had another dentist's injection. Although he'd ripped it to anger his parents, he couldn't help being frightened of what his father would do when he found it. It might take more than one bad deed to get sent home. It might take many more beatings...

"You are very quiet," said Sau. "Are you not excited to be meeting your family?"

"I'm confused," Low confessed. "There're so many Tangs in Britain."

"No, no, your uncle is not a Tang. He is a Haw." His mother screwed up her face as she endeavoured to explain the complicated relationships. "Your great-grandfather Tang had two children. Your father's father and your father's aunt. It was this aunt who married a Haw. After they came to England, they had one son. That is your uncle Haw."

"So today," said Low. "I will meet Uncle and Aunt Haw, and Great-Aunt and Great-Uncle Haw."

"No," his mother corrected, patiently. "Your Great-Aunt and Great-Uncle Haw died some years ago."

Low heaved a sigh of relief. The fewer Haws the better, he reckoned.

"But Great-Grandfather Tang still lives. He, also, looks forward to meeting you."

"I don't believe it!" exclaimed Low. "He must be ancient!"

"That is not polite," said his father.

"But he *is* very old," said his mother, a twinkle in her eyes. "Come here, Kitty, you must sit in your seat now."

Kitty had other ideas. She headed off down the lane, her little legs confident on the rough gravel. Low ran after her. He thought he'd soon catch her up, but she looked behind, giggled and ran all the faster. They were a long way from the car when he finally caught her. He whipped her up into his arms and spun her round and round. He knew small children loved this treatment. Kitty screamed with pleasure. As he put her gently down, she put her arms round his neck and implored, "Again!"

But his father was waving impatiently. Low lifted Kitty into his arms and carried her back. Her small, warm body held on to him tightly. As they proceeded down the lane, he remembered the boy he'd met here the previous night.

"Mother," Low asked, as Sau took the little girl from him. "Where does the Chinese family live?"

"I told you, in the centre of town."

"No, not our relations, the Chinese family who live near here. I met their son in this lane."

"We are the only Chinese family in Littlecoot," said his mother.

Low remembered the look of puzzlement that the boy had given when he'd asked him which house he lived in. "Perhaps he was just visiting, like we are, today," he said.

Low recognized the restaurant instantly as they pulled up outside. It was just as it had been in the photograph, with huge Chinese characters adorning one side of the building.

"The House of Haw," read Low.

"It's known as the best Cantonese restaurant in all the South West," said his father, a note of pride in his voice.

Low climbed out of the car, conscious of the silken feel of his very best clothes, as his aunt and uncle came forward to greet them. His aunt was full of kisses for Kitty. She took Low to her and hugged him too. His uncle was more formal. He gave a low bow, and ushered them through the restaurant, its many tables neatly laid with white cloths and napkins in wine glasses. They went into the family's rooms.

"And this is your great-grandfather Tang," his uncle said, taking Low by his reluctant shoulders and manoeuvring him over to the corner by the fireside.

Low looked down. His great-grandfather seemed shrunken half away, his wizened crab-apple face seemingly balanced on the collar of his stiff, dragon-embroidered jacket. From his upper lip and chin grew wisps of long white hair but his scalp was as smooth and bald as the knobs of Low's bedstead. A maroon satin cap warmed the very top of it. He was so thin, so fragile, that Low was afraid to touch him. Instead, he bowed deeply.

"Honourable Great-Grandfather," he said.

Suddenly, a vein-traced, insect-like claw shot out from inside the wide jacket sleeve. It clasped itself round Low's wrist and urged him forward. He was pulled so close he could feel his great-grandfather's kneecaps, like stone-hard mushrooms, digging against his legs.

"You came on the aeroplane?"

The question made Low start. There was no doubt that Great-Grandfather Tang had spoken, for his white moustache had flickered. But it seemed out of place, somehow. A question you would ask after many other, formal exchanges had taken place.

"Er...yes," said Low, looking round for support. But the others all suddenly seemed busy. His mother and aunt had disappeared into the kitchen to attend to the food, and Uncle Haw was on his hands and knees making Kitty chortle with laughter. His father had buried his head in a Chinese newspaper.

"I, too, came to England that way. It is remarkable, is it not, the shortness of such a journey?"

Low thought back to the flight, which at the time had seemed long enough, and then to the map in the geography lesson. For the first time, he realized just how far away from his home he was, and tears sprang into his eyes, hot and hateful.

"Fetch a stool to me, Low Hee, and tell me if my daughter-in-law is well."

Low took his time getting the three-legged stool. He had to work out who the old man was talking about – his mother had told him that both the old man's son and daughter were dead, so who was his daughter-in-law? Then he remembered what Grandmother had told him, months and miles ago. By the time he got back, he could say with confidence, "My grandmother was well when I left her." He'd got rid of the tears, hurriedly, into his jacket sleeve.

"Ee Tsang wrote to me, telling me of your voyage," said the old man, as Low settled on the stool. Then, almost to himself he added, "I have seen ninety-four New Years since my birth. I have not seen Malaysia for more than forty of them."

"But you wanted to come, didn't you?" urged Low.

"My son needed many able hands to build up his new English restaurant. I came to help him. That is why I am here."

Low saw himself, an old man, sitting close to a fire in a still-strange land, dreaming of the country he left so many years ago. His breathing came fast. He looked into his great-grandfather's dark sockets and gripped the stool.

"Couldn't you go back?" he asked, quietly. "If you liked?"

Ly Ah gave him a slow look. "I am too old for travel. I cannot walk."

"You don't have to walk when you go on a plane," said Low, into the hair round an ear. "I hate it here. We could go back together."

"No," came the reply. For several moments the old man was silent, deep in his own thoughts. Then, from behind the long white moustaches came a question.

"What is the second of the four noble truths?"

Low gave a little jolt. It was so long since he had thought about religious matters that he had to search his memory for the answer.

"Suffering is due to selfishness," he quoted, at last.

The skull made a small nod of approval. "You

suffer, Low Hee, because that is your desire. You wish to keep something that is no longer yours to keep. No one can feel happiness and hatred at the same time. It is not possible. You must swallow down your selfish desires to obtain happiness. In life, it is always up to the person. So the Buddha taught."

Crouched down on the three-legged stool, Low's eyes were at a level with Great-Grandfather Tang's. Low was strongly reminded of a corpse he'd once seen in a funeral procession. Ly Ah Tang's skin was tight and shiny over his skull, and his eyes were shrunken away into deep cavities. But Low saw them shine and glance about and gaze fully at him. The eyes, shrouded by their sockets, were still very alive.

"I don't understand," he said, finally.

"That is your own choice," said Ly Ah, maddeningly. He took Low's hand in his own claw. "And now, my smallest son, tell me about Malaysia."

CHAPTER NINE

"Low Hee...stop it...you are pulling me..."

Black shadows in grey haze.

An endless panorama of shapeless shadows. No pathway, no floor, no exit, no entrance.

"Low Hee...*stop it*..."

The face came towards him, out of the greyness. It shone like a circle of moonstone in the dull orange glow from a lamp. The dark eyes examined him curiously. When it was close enough to touch, Low put out his hand.

The glowing roundness bobbed away, shying from the touch, like a balloon on a current of air. Was it disembodied, Low wondered, or did the greyness hide everything but the pale flesh?

Without thinking it, Low knew he was dreaming. Although he was standing – his feet suspended an unknown distance above an invisible floor – he could feel the lumps of the mattress pushing against his back.

He lowered his arm and the face bobbed back.

It was the boy from the lane.

"You are pulling me," the boy whispered, in twangy Cantonese. "Please don't. I ought to go back, really, I know I should."

"I'm not touching you," Low hissed. "Go, then; go!"

"Calling me...you call me...all the time."

"I don't even know your name." At the back of his thoughts, a terror was growing. He should run from this place. But Low could not move his legs. There was no pathway, no floor, no desire. He was transfixed, like a rabbit in a beam of light. He could only stare at the bobbing face.

"My name is Liang...what is it...that makes you call?"

"I DON'T CALL YOU!"

The face bobbed away again, as though the loud anger in Low's words had frightened it. From the darkness and out of sight, Low heard it mutter.

"Your heart is weeping...like mine. I can tell. I know when a heart weeps like mine. We both want to go back. And we can't."

For a long moment, Low could not recall what was making him sad. He knew he was in pain, angry and miserable. But why, when his life was such a good one – a life full of sweet coconuts and pineapples ready for the picking, of festivals and sunshine. Then, like a rent in a piece of fine silk, the take-away shop, the boys at school and his father's grim mouth moved across the dark horizon. A feeling of nausea oozed into his stomach. Why did he have to remember?

"What are you sad about?" he asked the boy from the lane, in an effort to erase the tortured images.

"I've got to go to a new land," came the reply.

"I did that," Low sympathized.

"On a boat, across the biggest sea imaginable. It's a long journey, and I don't want to go."

"I don't want to stay."

"Stay here?" asked the disembodied face.

"I don't mean here," said Low. "Where is here, anyway?"

"It's a sort of nowhere, I think," said the boy. "A place you can fly to. You can't fall, look!" Instantly, he soared upward.

Low gazed up at him. I could do that, he thought, but his feet were stuck. He couldn't move them at all.

"It's easy," said the boy, from his elevation. "Beats having to walk, or climb. We had to climb down the cliff in the dark. It was awful, my hands got so cold I couldn't feel for handholds...down, down, down...it went on for ever. Father said, don't look down, but I could see the lamp on the boat out of the corner of my eye and that's when I missed a foothold and my hands slipped and I started to fall..."

"I thought you said you couldn't fall," said Low.

"That was before I came here. It's only here that you can fly about, I think. Come on," the boy called out, quite gaily. "Try it!"

He's pulling *me*, now, Low thought, and then, without knowing why, he thought: we pull each other.

Resolutely he worked at his legs, trying to draw

them loose. He let his mind relax and stepped out into the void.

But it was a false step – he was falling, not flying – the boy was wrong, you *could* fall from this place – the shadows and the face disappeared as he sailed downwards...

With a stifled cry, Low's eyes flew open. Yes, he'd been falling, but it was only the dream. You cannot fall if you are solidly lying on your mattress.

Yet something had fallen, and he was sure it was his heart, for he was nearly awake when it landed, thumping into place below his ribs, where it thumped now, fast and strong.

Low dragged his legs over the side of the bed and sat up. Immediately, the chill air made him shiver. His school uniform lay ready for the morning at the foot of his bed. He reached for the navy jumper and pulled it on. The floor was an iceberg which he had to walk across. When he got to the window, his teeth were working like pistons. He rubbed away the frosty coating and looked down. The lamp in the lane was out. Everything was misty grey, and the trees and bushes were dark, shapeless shadows.

Like the boy in his dream, Low was muttering to himself. It was nearly morning, and Low knew what the morning would bring.

"I've got to go to the Unit, and hand in the maths book, and the teacher will beat me, or maybe the headmaster, and my father will beat me and send me to bed hungry. But I've got to do it, because if they don't find out, they won't send me home."

"*Your selfish desires are the cause of your suffering.*" His great-grandfather's cracked tones echoed.

Suddenly, as he stared out at the steel-cold dawning of a March morning, he realized that he understood what the old man had meant. The beliefs his grandmother had drummed into him fell into perspective.

"People are selfish, and that's what stops them from finding the happiness of heaven. They go on being born, life after life, because they cannot put their own desires away. And life is suffering," Low whispered, repeating his grandmother's words. "So selfish desires are the cause of suffering."

"But why should it be me who's the selfish one?" asked Low. "Father was selfish, bringing me here. Why does no one consider that? Why should it be so wrong for me to want to go?"

"I don't want to go," Liang had told him, as he'd floated above him. Nirvana, thought Low – the heaven that Buddha promised his followers – was supposed to be an empty place, devoid of suffering, devoid of desire. Was it a place you could float to in a dream? Had he and Liang had a heavenly taste of Nirvana?

That couldn't be possible, he told himself, you only get to Nirvana after many reincarnations. It had only been somewhere in a strange dream.

Wherever they had been, it was better than this

English city. Anywhere was better than this English city. Anywhere in the world.

Low leant his back against the icy panes of the window and let the tears flow freely in the dark privacy of his room.

CHAPTER TEN

The Remedial Unit was a small classroom at the end of a corridor. Low arrived on Monday morning with bitterness on his face and in his heart. He would be nice to no one, learn nothing and speak only Cantonese. He kept repeating to himself, "I *will* go home. I *will*." He gave the door a hard push which was almost a slam and scowled at the class. He took in the gaily-covered walls, the large, square tables, the cage in the corner with a small, tan creature asleep inside, the eleven other pupils and Miss Hale at her desk.

It was then he saw the sun bird.

Long ago, a lifetime ago, he'd done a project in school on a tiny Malaysian bird with feathers in all the colours of Paradise. He thought he would never see anything more beautiful, until today.

On a chair by Miss Hale sat a human sun bird. A girl as slender as a chopstick, with creamy skin framed by a black curtain of hair that swung in a carefree fashion each time she moved her head. She sported sun bird attire, feathery folds of vibrant cloth billowing out from her arms and legs, brilliant shades of purple and pink, yellow and crimson. She might have stepped straight out of the forests of South East Asia.

The vision of splendour smiled at Low and his

dark scowl couldn't help but soften.

"Low," called Miss Hale. "Come here, please."

Low had not been going to comply with any English instructions that morning, but on seeing the sun bird girl, the words shouting in his mind, "I *will* go home," had quietened to a whisper. Slowly, he walked over to the desk.

"This is Miss Kung, Low," said the teacher, and for a moment they spoke together in English. Low gawped, unable to prevent admiration of her flawless command of the tongue welling up.

Then she turned to him and spoke again, this time, in perfect Cantonese.

"Good morning, Low. How are you?"

Low's feelings of isolation melted away. "You're from Malaysia!" he cried.

"No, I'm from Hong Kong," smiled Miss Kung. "But as you can hear we both speak the same language. Isn't that a good beginning?"

For a moment, Low felt lost for words, but as Miss Hale led them to a table away from the others, he began to bombard the girl with questions.

"Where have you come from? Not all the way from Hong Kong, surely? Are you here just for me? So that I have someone to talk to?"

The sun bird laughed. "No, I haven't come all the way from Hong Kong. I've lived here ever since I was a little girl. I'm a student at the university, now. I study design. Look, I designed the clothes I'm wearing!" With a neat movement she rose from her seat and twirled herself round like a multi-coloured spinning top. Low's head was filled with colour and laughter and excitement. Everyone in the room was looking at the girl.

"Last week," she went on, "I had a message through the language department that this school needed someone who could speak Cantonese. In the whole university, I was chosen to help you!"

Low remembered his manners and gave a bow. "This is most kind."

She gave her curtain of hair a shake. "Anyone would do the same; I expect you will one day. Please call me Sue, by the way, I hate being called Miss Kung."

"Sue," said Low, wonderingly, "does this mean I can have lessons in Cantonese, now?"

Sue exploded into giggles. "Believe me – I'm no teacher. The only thing I was ever good at was art. Besides, I can't stay all day. I'll come three mornings a week, to help you learn English."

Low didn't reply. His face darkened again.

"Is something wrong?" asked Sue. "Please, tell me what it is."

Low reached into his bag and drew out the ruined maths book. He lay it on the table, unable to speak, knowing the book spoke more clearly of his misery than he could.

"You...you did this?" Sue asked.

Low nodded.

"Why?"

Sue listened while Low told her, bit by bit, about his grandmother and his life in Malaysia. About his resolution to waste no time in getting back. But Low could not tell even a gaily-painted sun bird everything. He knew it would be disloyal to mention the fear he had of his father, or the reasons he had for it. When he'd finished, Sue raised her beautiful face and smiled a tiny smile.

"Why did your parents not bring you when they first came?"

"Grandmother said it was because they had nowhere to live and no money. But they had my sister, Kitty! They managed to keep her."

Sue shrugged. "Perhaps they had no choice."

"They left me when I was only a little boy," said Low, looking down at the maths book. "At first, I couldn't remember them at all. And now, I can't forget my grandmother."

"You are homesick," Sue observed.

"Were you...homesick...when you first came?"

Sue nodded. "But I was with my parents. We all had each other, in this strange country, to remind us of the old one. As the years went on, Hong Kong became just a memory and this place became home." Sue paused for a moment, as if weighing her words.

"I think, Low, that you imagine you have left behind everyone that loves you. But I'm sure that's not true. I'm sure your mum and dad love you, really. You don't know each other properly, yet, that's all. You're all strangers, meeting in a strange land. You'll have to be patient and willing to get to know each other, all over again."

"But why do I have to?" asked Low. "What's so wrong with going back?"

"None of us can move backwards," said Sue. "That's the wrong way to live your life. You have to look ahead."

"That's what my great-grandfather said."

"He was right," said Sue. Then she added, more thoughtfully, "Your great-grandfather, does he live in England?"

"He lives at The House of Haw."

"Really? In the centre of Bristol?"

"You know it?" asked Low.

"I've eaten there. Wonderful Cantonese cooking!"

Low grinned. "My great-grandfather hated it here when he first came. He told me."

"It's hard to settle down at first," said Sue. "Sometimes the old people understand that best."

As she spoke, she slid the maths book towards her. "I'll explain this to Miss Hale for you," she said. "Now, let's translate the timetable she's given me into Cantonese."

Towards the end of the morning, she brought to their table a boy with untidy hair the colour of field mice. When Low rose to greet him in polite oriental manner, he noticed that he was not tall for an English boy, hardly any taller than Low.

"This is Tristam," said Sue. "Miss Hale

suggested he might look after you a bit. You two have a chat, and I'll act as interpreter."

Low thought up some questions just to please Sue. He discovered that Tristam lived ten minutes' walk from the school, and that he had two older brothers and a younger sister.

Once Tristam started chattering, there was no stopping him. Sue had a busy time translating everything he was saying.

"It's me favourite thing, s'afternoon. Swimming lessons. Are you doing it?" he asked Low. "Have you brought your kit?"

"Kit?" Low replied. "Whatever d'you need to go swimming? Surely you just jump in and swim!"

Sue laughed. "Yes, and in the tropics you can just climb out and dry off in the sun. Over here you need boring things like trunks and towels."

"I can get you a spare kit," said Tristam, when he'd learnt what the problem was. "I can bring it back with me when I go home for dinner. We've got masses of spare clothes in our house," he confided. "'Cause our mum never throws anything out. First Robert wears things, then Adam does, then me. Sometimes they even get passed down to me sister if our mum reckons there's any wear left in them."

Low asked him what the Unit was like.

"I hate school," he replied. "But the Unit is nicer than the juniors, 'cause I was at the bottom of my class in year six but I'm not here. I'm getting better at reading. I still hate maths, though!"

"You could help Tristam with his maths," Sue pointed out, slyly, "if you could speak more of his language."

Low looked away. Sue's eyes were always full of a sincerity which was half hidden away under constant, bubbling merriment. But under that again, he recognized strong determination. He had a feeling that he would never get home if he co-operated. His only chance was to make a fuss, yet even breaking up a textbook had so far got him nowhere.

Low had persuaded his mother to make him a packed lunch, and he spent the dinner hour roaming the school grounds, picking at bits of spring roll.

The wind chased him round the sides of buildings, turning his fingers and ears to ice and reminding him that the chill of loneliness went right to the bone.

Finally, he spotted Tristam, waving and running towards him, carrier bags in either hand.

"Couldn't find you for ages," he said, all out of breath. "I got the trunks, look, they're an old pair of Robert's, but they've got a string inside them so you can tighten them up. And I brought a towel." He took the things out of their bag and waved them at Low.

"TRUNKS! TOWEL!"

"I'm not deaf," snapped Low in his own language. But the feeling of sourness couldn't last long, with Tristam's happy nattering going on all the time. He hadn't chosen the boy to be his mate, but the wide grin Tristam displayed made him realize he should try to be friendly.

"Can you swim?" asked the boy, making breast-stroke movements. "SWIM?"

"Sim," Low said, nodding. The trouble with pretending he didn't understand anything was that it made him look stupid and Low hated to look *that*. "Yeh. Sim."

"Good?" asked Tristam, changing to free-stroke.

"Yeh. Sim. Good."

The repugnant language was coming to him, despite his loathing of it.

Tristam looked at his watch. "We gotta go." He snatched at Low's sleeve to instruct him to follow and raced off in the direction of the swimming pool, Low right behind. They pushed at the heavy door and went inside. A feeling of humid warmth, the smell of chlorine and the echoing sounds of boys laughing and chatting hit him.

"Sim?"

"Yeah, it's the pool. SWIMMING POOL!"

Low hated the way Tristam shouted. As if it would help him understand. Well, he didn't want to understand anyway. He felt cross with himself. If he wanted to get home fast, he would have to remember – not a word of English.

Tristam watched Low's expression change from friendly to unwelcoming. He knew nothing of

Low's inner struggles and wondered if this strange boy was worth the trouble he was taking with him. "OK, be like that," he muttered to himself, seeing Low turn away and find an empty corner to change in.

Low struggled into the gaily coloured trunks and tightened the string. They felt a bit odd, but he decided he'd soon get used to them. He wandered out of the changing rooms. He was the only person on the pool side but it didn't occur to him that the others were waiting for the teacher's go-ahead.

The expanse of green ripples, breaking and bending the black lines below, beckoned to him. He had only once before swum in a pool, when Koong's family had taken him with them to the nearest big city for a short holiday. He was used to murk and mud and waterfowl and passing shoals of tiny fish. He was used to watching out for fast currents and other dangers, the menacing eyes of the occasional submerged crocodile.

He dangled one toe into the deep end to test the temperature. Then he raised his arms and bent his knees into the posture of a diver.

He felt a pressure on his spine. The push propelled him forward, his dive precipitated by the force. He hit the water at a bad angle, his nose and mouth filling with the taste of chlorine. He felt, rather than heard, another splash break the surface.

He bobbed upwards. As he looked round to locate the second swimmer, a grip tightened on the back of his shoulders. Heavy pressure pushed him down until the coolness of the water surrounded him.

Through the distortions of light and sound Skiff's face, now near, now distant, flickered in the turquoise water. Low saw an expression filled with malevolent delight.

Skiff was almost on top of him now, the full weight of his own body holding Low below the surface, his hands gripping Low's shoulders tightly.

It didn't occur to Low to struggle free. He was used to underwater fun. At home, he'd often scrapped with his mates in the reed-infested Malaysian rivers. Now, he used those old skills to cartwheel over in the water, gripping at his opponent's wrists to prevent them moving closer to his throat. He pulled at Skiff, locking the boy's legs into his, urging him down. They spiralled round and round in the natural buoyancy of the water, the weight of their locked bodies and the currents they created by their spin propelling them away from the surface until Low felt the slippery shine of tiles against his bare back.

In the strange silence of this displaced, floating world, Low was the aggressor. He held Skiff captive, keeping his tight grip round his wrists and legs. The kicks Skiff aimed at Low with his knees and feet were ineffectual. Bubbles escaped from his half-closed mouth. When Low felt the urgent jerkings of real panic course through Skiff's body, he let loose his grasp.

Skiff shot to the surface, arms and legs flapping. Low gave himself a push-up from the tiles and rose more smoothly.

He hit the surface and took in his first breath. He shook the stinging water out of his eyes and focused quickly upon Skiff, alert to a second attack.

There was a crowd by the pool. Arms were reaching down for Skiff, pulling him out of the water. Low recognized Tristam, who was waving and calling.

Low struck out for the side. Tristam offered his hand and Low swung up with a single movement. He looked down and saw Skiff, on hands and knees, a towel over his hunched shoulders. He coughed repeatedly, and a tall man in a navy tracksuit was supporting the heaving shoulders.

"Ah, the other offender," said the man. He turned for a moment towards Low, his face grim. "Perhaps you'll be able to offer some explanation for this."

"Sir, he can't understand you!"

"He doesn't speak English, Mr Barrow!"

The teacher sighed. Skiff took in a full, shuddering lungful of air.

"No doubt they'll both have plenty to say later," said Mr Barrow, and added, as Tristam came bounding up with the towel he'd brought for Low, "Don't *run*, boy!"

Low took the towel from Tristam and pulled it

gratefully round his shoulders.

"You said you were a good swimmer," Tristam affirmed, "but I didn't really believe you. Not *that* good." He turned to the assembled crowd. "I thought he would be *dead* when he came up!"

The replies Low heard coming from the other boys were meaningless, but he could detect admiration in their voices.

"He wasn't even breathless!"

"He was down there longer than Skiff!"

"Brilliant swimmer."

"Yeah. Major event."

"Got to have him in the team, sir."

Skiff at last struggled to his feet. He looked Low's way, his eyes burning with hate, his lips a nasty purplish shade. "...You...Chink!" he spat. He turned to Mr Barrow. Words fell from his lips like rough stones. His looks and gestures singled Low out from the silent, listening crowd.

Low didn't have to understand Skiff's barrage of stony words to know he was lying. It was obvious he would make what he could of his opportunity, knowing Low couldn't defend himself.

It's not fair, Low thought. Why should I have to be here, in this awful place, among these heartless people?

His life was a mess now, out of control.

He looked down at the sloping sides of the pool. Down there, he thought, he had almost enjoyed himself. Just for a moment, he had been in control –

in an environment that he knew how to handle...warm, silent, equal. It took all his willpower to walk away from the pool, back to the changing rooms. He longed to float to the bottom again.

CHAPTER ELEVEN

They stood side by side in the headmaster's office, Skiff grinning, Low scowling. Skiff voluble, Low silent.

For one tiny second, Low imagined how much better things would be if he could speak to the man who sat behind the desk wearily turning a fountain pen over and over in his hands. If he could speak the language, he could explain his side of things. He buried the thought, fast and hard.

"We could do with that girl from the university," said Mr Trenchard, looking at Low in despair. "But she won't be back until Wednesday."

"Well, you ask her this when she comes, then," said Skiff, breathing hard. "Ask her to ask him if he didn't kick me in the chin last week, hard enough to knock me flying. You ask her that. Violent, he is! He's out to kill me."

The headmaster picked up the phone and dialled Tang's Take-Away. It took Low a few minutes to realize what he was doing. He didn't have much experience of phones. When he heard his father's name spoken, he lurched forward, almost falling, and clutched the edge of the office desk for support.

Mr Trenchard spoke for a few moments. His voice was calm and it was clear that he was trying to be fair, asking his father to help with a translation of

Low's side of things. He gestured to Low, presenting him with the telephone, pushing it towards him.

Low looked at Mr Trenchard, his eyes huge with terror. He'd only spoken a few times on a phone before, but he knew that his father must be waiting at the other end, ready to question him.

"Go on, boy," said the headmaster, impatience creeping into his voice.

Low put the receiver gingerly to his ear.

"What is this all about, Low Hee?" he heard his father say in clipped tones.

"Father..."

"Son of Tang disgraces the family name by getting into trouble."

"I only defended myself..."

"When you get home, we will talk."

The receiver buzzed in his ear. He pulled it away and looked into it, perplexed. His father had hung up.

After Skiff and he had been dismissed to their classes, Skiff flashed a look of triumph at Low, and dashed off, his trainers skidding as he rounded the first corner.

Low wandered the corridors. He could still occasionally take the wrong turning. He'd found the Unit easily enough that morning, but now it eluded him. The corridors looked more alien than ever. He was walking in a part of the school he hadn't seen before. He looked at his watch. The day was nearly over, anyhow, only an hour before the final bell.

"...When you get home, we will talk..."

Wye Liew was angry, Low could well tell. He resigned himself to the fear that swelled in his stomach. He would gladly take the anger, and the punishment that would follow, if, after all of it, his father would resolve to send him back to Malaysia. Surely, now he had disgraced the family name, they wouldn't want him any more.

"...When you get home, we will talk..."

Low slipped out through a side door. He was at the back of the school. A wide expanse of playing field stretched before him.

Without a coat, the March wind struck cold. He began to run across the boggy grass without really knowing where he was heading.

Except that it was away. Away from Skiff, the Unit, his father.

He was breathless by the time he reached the far side of the playing fields. He stopped to gain his breath.

On the other side of the high wire fence, the traffic roared. He didn't recognize this main road at all.

"I should go back," he told himself. "Before I'm missed. Before the home-bell."

"...When you get home..."

Low gave a short, spitting laugh. Home? His father called it home?

Home was a place of warmth, sunshine and love, laughter and fun. He had no home in this land.

He pushed himself under the curling base of the wire fence and walked along the road. A group of people were standing together near the kerb. As he gained on them, a gaily painted minibus drew up. Low watched as the people filed on. He stopped for a moment. His fingers touched the change in the depths of his trouser pocket.

He ran to the back of the queue.

A round, middle-aged woman in a raincoat stood in front of him. He tapped her on the arm.

"Scus, pliss...Bis-tol?" he enquired, urgently.

"What? I'm sorry?"

For the second time that afternoon, he cursed his lack of English.

"Go...Bis-tol?"

"What's he saying?" said the woman to a younger woman in front. "D'YOU WANT THIS BUS?" she added, speaking slowly but so loudly that Low took a step back.

"P'raps he wants to know where it goes," said the younger woman, scrabbling in a big shoulder-bag for her purse.

"I can't understand a word," said the first woman. "Chinese or something."

"P'raps he's on an exchange."

"He's young to be on his own."

"Well...they're independent, aren't they?"

All this time, the queue moved in fits and starts towards the mouth of the bus.

"The House of Haw?" Low tried in slow

Cantonese. Then again, "BIS-TOL?"

"He wants the centre, I expect. Needs to meet someone there, or something. BRISTOL CITY CENTRE? OR THE BUS STATION?"

Low nodded, frantically. Now they were on the first step of the bus entrance. "Bis-tol. Haw."

"HAVE YOU GOT THE FARE?" The woman in the raincoat waved her purse at Low.

Low pulled some coins from his pocket and held them out. The woman pointed to a fifty-pence coin. "You'll need all of that. Look, I'll ask for you, love."

They entered the bus. Low hovered by the automatic doors, while the woman spoke to the driver.

"He wants the centre, or something...keeps asking for Bristol. 'Spect that's what he means, don't you?"

The driver leant forward, raising his voice. "You want the centre, mate? Bristol centre?"

"Bis-tol," said Low. He pocketed the ticket offered him and slid into a seat. The woman in the raincoat sat next to him.

"Where are you going, then, love?" she asked, concerned. "STATION? TRAIN? BUS?"

Low stared. None of the words meant anything. "Haw?" he asked, hopefully.

"What's Haw, love? That your name?"

Low turned his head and stared through the window. This is stupid, he thought to himself. What am I doing? I'll be lost in this cold land, I should get off, find my way back.

The bus jogged and jerked its way into town. Low stared hard from the windows, trying to build up a picture in his mind of the journey he'd taken the previous day. What route had his father taken, to get to The House of Haw?

They passed an imposing grey building with majestic turrets.

"THIS IS THE TRAIN STATION, LOVE," shouted the woman, pointing, "D'YOU WANT THE TRAINS?"

Low gave the woman a grim smile and shook his head. "Haw," he said again, but his voice was shaky. He was surprised at how close he was to tears. He breathed deeply and tried to maintain an inscrutable expression.

They reached the shopping centre and the bus slowed as it pushed its way through the traffic. Its doors opened, exchanged its passengers, closed again. The shops were enormous, the crowds of people overwhelming.

Then, as they swung round a corner and picked up speed, Low saw the restaurant. The enormous Chinese characters called out to him.

The House of Haw.

Low let out a cry, shot from his seat and pushed past the lady in the raincoat.

"Haw!" he told her. He made for the driver's cab. "Pliss..."

"I think he wants to get off, driver," said his companion.

"He'll have to wait for the bus stop, then, like the rest of us, won't he?" sang the driver.

The bus rattled on. Low lost sight of the sign, the restaurant, the street. They turned yet another corner.

"Pliss..." whispered Low, softly.

At last the driver pulled the bus into the kerb and brought it to a halt. Low jumped out. His step was light as he landed on the hard Bristol pavements. He felt pleased with himself. Luck had been with him for once.

For once, all was well.

Low put his head down and ran through the afternoon crowds towards The House of Haw.

CHAPTER TWELVE

"When the Holy Buddha was a young boy, he lived the charmed life of a prince," said Ly Ah Tang from behind his white whiskers. "He played in the fields with his friends, learnt combat and sport with them, lay drowsing in the hot sun whenever he wished. He had no work except school work, and this was probably tedious to him. No doubt he gazed out of the window instead, dreaming of the laughter and fun he would have when lessons were over. Now, my great-grandson, does that remind you of anyone?"

Once again, Low crouched on the three-legged stool and gazed into his great-grandfather's rheumy eyes. The fire blazed before them both, roasting Low's cheeks pleasantly. Low thought about the question Ly Ah had posed. Who could the Prince Buddha possibly resemble?

"Why, it reminds me of no one, Great-Grandfather," he said.

He heard a wheezy chuckle build up in Ly Ah's chest and explode from his lips. His long whiskers flicked like rodents' tails. "It should remind Low of himself! That's what it should do! Low Hee has lived a charmed life full of happy, careless pleasures. How do I know that? Because my esteemed daughter-in-law wrote many times describing her life with you.

And because you told me yourself, when I saw you...when was it?"

"Only yesterday, Great-Grandfather."

"But tell me, Low, what happened to the Buddha?"

These were the tales Low had learnt from his grandmother. He knew them well. "The Buddha went out in his chariot one day and saw...he saw..."

"What did he see, Low?"

"Suffering and disease and...er...death..."

He hadn't wanted to upset Ly Ah, so old and obviously near to death himself.

"No life can be lived without pain and suffering," said Ly Ah, almost to himself. He rocked himself gently back and forth in his stiff-backed chair. "But all things pass...every act has its own result..."

"What are you saying, Great-Grandfather?" whispered Low. "That I had all my pleasures at once? And now they're over for ever – from now on, only pain?"

But Ly Ah had a perplexing way of sinking into himself at times, leaving questions unanswered, and drifting off. Low supposed it was to do with being so very old. He shifted on the hard stool and kept silent.

"You have been sorely tried and tempted," said his great-grandfather, finally. "But you kept to the path and for that I commend you. You used the Right Conduct, defending yourself with honour against this...Skiff. You resisted the temptation of retaliation. That was correct."

Low's cheeks darkened. He was grateful for the burning heat of the fire which masked his discomfort. He had not told Ly Ah the whole of it, about skipping school early, and the telephone call with his father.

"...*When you get home...*"

Low had arrived at The House of Haw breathless from the run. Straight away, his uncle had asked, "How is it you have come on your own?"

And Low had replied, "I came on the bus. My father gave me the money," which was true, but only in a false way.

Aunt Haw had said, "But why did he not bring you in the car?"

And Low had replied, "He values independence in a son. Also, he could not spare the time." This wasn't a lie, but it wasn't the truth, either.

Great-Grandfather Tang had called from his corner, "Let the boy alone, Su Ying. Bring him to me. I wish to speak with him." Low wondered now, watching the drowsing, nodding head, how much the old man had guessed.

But none of this was the burning thing, which consumed Low's spirit like the fire which consumed the logs that fell and spat in the grate. Low leant forward, seeking the old man's wire-haired ear.

"When I was down there, Great-Grandfather, down there at the bottom of the pool, I mean, I had a strange feeling. It reminded me of a dream I had last night."

Ly Ah rocked. "What was that dream?"

"I was floating, as though in water, but there wasn't any water, it was a shapeless place, without floors or walls. There was a boy – I'd seen him before – he could float up and down and spin around. He said he'd flown there – no – that he'd fallen, from a cliff. He said...I'd called him."

"Where had you seen this boy before, Low Hee?"

"In the lane behind our shop. He is the strangest boy! He wears traditional clothes all the time, but they are not silk. They're rough cloth, and ragged. I suppose because he wears them all the time.

"He frightens me, a bit," Low added, without meaning to. Liang's bewildered expression scared him far more than Skiff's foxy grin ever could. "I don't know...is it my imagination...or what?"

"The monks of the Sagma would tell you never to be afraid of your dreams," said Ly. "Your soul is attached to your body. You cannot lose it. If you wander away from yourself in a dream, there is a silver cord which will always bring you back."

"D'you mean," Low almost whispered, "that you can get out of your body somehow? And come back again after? D'you mean that I met that boy's *soul*?"

"Uh-huh," grunted the nodding head. Low took hold of a mushroom-cap knee and shook it in an effort to keep his grandfather awake.

"D'you mean," Low went on, "that I wandered away from myself? To that place? You mean I went somewhere, in my dream?"

"Who knows?" replied his great-grandfather, in his perplexing manner. "Only you can tell that."

"How can I?"

"If the dream recurs," said his great-grandfather in his thin squeak of a voice, "ask yourself that question then. If you can answer, it will tell you many things."

"If it was true," said Low, "that I went away from myself last night, it would explain the feeling I had as I woke."

"You felt yourself rush back? Back into your body?"

"Yes," said Low, from between clenched teeth. Ly Ah's words were not reassuring him. He felt more lost than ever. "Why is this happening to me?" asked Low. He had sometimes wondered if it was anything to do with all his miseries, the changes in his life, the new bed, the new room, the new land. "Is it...real?"

"What is 'real' in the world?" muttered Ly Ah. Low heard a rumbling from his chest. The old man was chuckling with merriment. It was all right for him, Low thought bitterly. He could sit by his fire in his chair. His life was over.

"What happens if the silver cord snaps?" whispered Low.

"It never could. Unless your body is preparing for death. Unless your soul longs to leave your body. It seeks out the great light and leaves the body behind as if it were nothing but an old suit of clothes."

"Does that scare you sometimes, honourable father?"

"No," chuckled Ly Ah. "I've been wearing this old body for too many years now. What will be...I am ready for."

"Low Hee." His uncle stood behind them. In his hand were his car keys. "Low Hee, I have just telephoned your father. He told me he didn't know you were here. He was worried about you. He has asked me to take you home."

"...When you get home, we will talk..."

Low looked quickly at Ly Ah,`but it was as if he hadn't heard his grandson speak. He seemed already asleep, his chin nodding down on to his breastbone. Low leant over and took the old man's bony fingers into his plump hand. Then he rose, and followed his uncle.

CHAPTER THIRTEEN

"And this is our menu," said Sau Kit, showing Low the painted board with a wave of her hand. "Everything we sell is on it – chow mein...foo yung...all the sweet and sours..."

Low leant against the counter, kicking it with the heel of his shoe. He beat out a rhythm, kicking in time to the chant in his head – I *will* go home...I *will* go home...

"You are listening to me, Low, aren't you?" Sau gave him her usual smile, but this afternoon it seemed painted on. "Repeat the words I say in English. Pan-cake-roll...sweet-n-sour..."

Low went on kicking the counter. The dishes at Tang's Take-Away were nothing like good Cantonese cooking. They had been scaled down, to make them affordable, his father had explained, to English purses. Low hadn't appreciated how delicious his grandmother's cooking was until he'd come here and eaten take-away food, which tasted of everything and yet of nothing as if the ingredients had been thrown together and ended up a mess.

"Low, stop that kicking, please," said Sau, through her painted smile. "All the dishes are numbered, see here? Some people ask for them by name, some by number. So you will have to learn the numbers too. Can you count in English, Low?"

Low shrugged. Stupid mother, he thought. Why ask stupid questions? "What d'you think?" he growled.

He knew he'd gone too far, been too discourteous, when his mother suddenly came towards him and began shouting in high, rapid English.

"What I think? I think I have fool for son! What you suppose it like for us when we first came here? Huh? What you think it like for us? Long hours we work, in some other Chinese take-way, ve' hard, learnin' to unda-san what people say – unda-san new money, new words – livin' in li'l room – so tiny – no cookin' 'lowed – savin' all money! Evely pound going to bank – what you think it was like – huh? Evely pound so we could get own take-way. So we could come get you – our son – get you here – home. This is home – unda-san?"

Low blinked. "I didn't understand you. I don't understand English," he said.

"No!" cried his mother, triumphantly in Cantonese. "You do not understand English, do you? But you will, because you will have to. That is why we have chosen not to punish you for your misbehaviour. Instead you will learn the language – and quickly!"

Low's heel beat out an angry rhythm. Things had not worked out as he'd planned. When he'd got back on Monday night with his uncle he'd been expecting shouts, yelled accusations, a sound beating with the bamboo stick that still lurked in the back yard.

Instead, he'd been sent to his room and no one had come near him until Uncle Haw had left. What seemed like hours later, his father walked slowly into the bedroom.

He'd looked dispirited rather than angry. He'd sunk on to the end of Low's bed and looked at Low for a long time before speaking. Low had not looked back.

At last he had said, "Why did you go to Great-Grandfather for advice? Instead of coming to me?"

Caught off guard, Low shook his head. "You wouldn't understand."

"Do you think I was never a boy?" Wye Liew replied, his voice rising. Low watched him struggle to regain his temper. "Tell me what is bothering you, Low, and see if I understand."

Low was tempted to grin. It would serve his father right if he did just that. All right, he thought. If that's what you want.

"I want to go home," he said.

"This is your home," countered his father. "Here with your mother, your sister and me."

Low shook his head again. "Never," he said. "Malaysia's my home. My grandmother's house is my home. I want to go back there."

"That is no way for a son to speak to his father," said Wye Liew. His breath was coming quickly and there were dangerous pinkish patches on his hollow cheeks.

"But you asked me," said Low. "You said, 'see if I understand'. And you don't."

"We have been apart too long," Wye Liew sounded sorrowful. Low gave him a quick glance, but his father was studying the faded bedspread. "I didn't mean for that to happen. I expected to come to England, buy a property then come and fetch you in less than a year. I didn't realize how hard it would be. How long we would have to save. And in the meantime, you were growing up. Into a boy I didn't know."

"You..." Low tried to put together the thing that had been on his mind since he'd first seen Tang's Take-Away. "You never came to visit me, or told me about Kitty."

"We couldn't afford the air fare," said his father. He didn't continue. Low wondered if there really was any good excuse for keeping the birth of his sister a secret. He couldn't think of one.

"We have been talking," his father went on. "Your mother, Uncle Haw and I. We were remembering what it was like to be here, in England, when we first arrived. We all agreed that once we'd learnt the language, it became easier, more pleasant. So we thought, how could Low learn English more quickly? And the answer was simple – the same way as we did!"

Low looked at his father for the first time. The words, so lightly spoken, sounded ominous. "How did you learn?" he asked.

"Through our jobs – there was no escape – we had to understand the take-away orders! You see? So simple!"

So what? thought Low.

"It was then I had my grand idea. From now on, you will help us serve in the shop. Not in the back, carrying and fetching. In the shop behind the counter. That way, you will learn quickly, as we did."

"Is this to be my punishment?" asked Low.

"There *is* no punishment," said Wye Liew. "Just a change in the pattern of things. You will learn so much! How to count, how to speak English, how to deal with the English money...you'll start tomorrow night. As soon as you get home from school, your mother will show you what to do. She will help you."

And now, his mother *was* helping him. She was pointing to the menu board and counting slowly, "One, two, three, four, repeat," said Sau.

"Wun...too...thee...um..." said Low.

"Four," said Sau.

Low looked at the clock. It was nearly opening time. His stomach churned. The smell of cooking made him feel sick.

"Seventeen...eighteen..." said his mother.

Like a green parrot, Low repeated everything. His stomach rolled over and over as the clock ticked on.

Sau took Low behind the counter and showed

him how to manage the chip-baskets, and the English fried food. "This is a heated cabinet," she explained. "A lot of the English like the fish. This is the fish. They will ask for 'fish-lot' or 'cod-lot' or a piece of cod, or cod and chips or fish and chips. Got that?"

"Yes," lied Low, the stomach-churning, clock-watching green parrot.

And suddenly, it was five o'clock.

CHAPTER FOURTEEN

Sau opened the doors and, at first, the customers only trickled in, one or two at a time. Sau stood next to Low, while Wye Liew ran about with hot food and buckets of raw chips. She smiled at each customer, spoke to them in English, took the order and translated it for Low. All she expected him to do was put up the right things. For the moment, that was enough, she explained.

Low got used to shovelling chips. He built up a speed, ignoring the spits from the hot oil and the sweat that dripped into his eyes. Sau was delighted.

"My ve' speedy son," she explained to customers. "He has learn English fast."

It was six o'clock when the first queue built up. As Sau and Low were serving some people who wanted a large Chinese order, a motorbike drew up outside Tang's Take-Away and a pair of bikers sauntered in, followed by another group of young people.

"Got any flaky pasties?" asked the bike-boy, staring into the heated cabinet.

There had been a run on flaky pasties. Sau said something to the boy in rapid English and turned to Low.

"I'll have to get some more out of the fridge and heat them in the microwave," she explained. "You can serve the next person. I'll take the money when I get back."

The next person was the bike-girl. She had long black hair, and was encased in leather from head to foot. She held her crash helmet under one arm.

"I want a cod-lot," she said. "Plenty of chips, please," she added, giving Low a wink.

"Tip?" Low replied, and sighed with relief at the simple order. He shovelled chips into greaseproof paper.

"Hey! Don't forget my cod!" smiled the girl.

Low glanced wildly the length of the cabinet. He pointed to a piece of battered cod. "Cod?" he queried.

"That's right!" said the girl. She was giggling good-naturedly, and laughed outright when, in his nervousness, Low picked up the cod with his hands and watched it fall apart as he carried it.

"Never mind," she said, as her order was bundled towards her.

Wiping his greasy, sweaty hands across his white apron, Low reluctantly turned to the next waiting group, who were chatting together and pointing to the menu board. He gave them a smile as stiff as sticks and said, "Yeh?"

"Yeah, right," said a tall boy from amongst them. "Er...we want...what was yours, Sal? Right. Two cod -lots, one with a pickled egg, one pork sweet'n'sour, one chicken chow mein, both with rice, and one crispy beef noodles with a portion of chips. Please."

Low's grin stayed in place, developing into a wide snarl of frozen terror.

"Tell him the numbers," said a girl in the group, after a silence. "From the menu."

"Oh, yeah," said the tall boy. He began to call out numbers. "Write them down then," he said to Low, waving his hand at the paper pad on the counter.

The place suddenly seemed filled with hungry, expectant people. The group who were waiting for the Chinese order, the bikers still waiting for the flaky pasty, the gang of young people, and now the door opened again and a man came in with his two children. Low's stomach rolled. He'd had nothing to eat since his packed lunch, but he felt sure he would be sick at any moment. He backed away from the staring eyes of the customers.

"You got that, then?" asked the tall boy.

"Yeh. Pliss." said Low. Without turning his back, he moved slowly towards the door that led into the cooking area. Suddenly, he shot through it, passing his mother and father and finding himself out in the yard before he really had an idea of what he was doing. He heard his father's call. He ran to the fence at the bottom of the yard, and scrambled up until he could see into the empty lane. No one was there.

"Low!" His father stood in the doorway, his thin body silhouetted against the yellow light of the kitchen.

Low turned slightly, using his arms and the toes

of his shoes to support his position. "I feel sick!" he called back. "I thought I was going to be sick!"

He watched his father step out into the yard. He seemed to glance around as if looking for something.

The bamboo stick! thought Low, and called out softly, "Liang..." As if the boy could do anything for his plight, he told himself cruelly. What was the good? And yet, as his father advanced across the concrete Low found himself suddenly springing into action. His shoes gripped the next foothold. He gave a big heave and lifted himself clear of the boards, balancing on the lip of the fencing.

"Low!" Now his father's voice was sharp with urgency. "Get down!"

Low knew his father could reach him, pull him down if he just ran a few, short strides. One good leap, though, and he'd be in the lane. He could just run...anywhere.

"LOW!" his mother's voice came in a long scream. As he jumped his toe caught behind him in the barbed wire; he plummeted – head first. He heard the scream, first and last. It lingered after everything else had blackened into night.

CHAPTER FIFTEEN

The glow from the lamp below him was a dull orange halo. Low saw it and wondered why was he above it. Had the fall so disorientated him that everything was topsy-turvy?

As he got used to the glare of the lamp, he saw below it the lane itself, a black ribbon of tarmac between the bushes and fences. Sprawled on the ground was a small figure, at first hardly discernible, except for a luminous square patch of white apron and the round, moon-glow of a face.

He recalled the first time he had seen Liang in the lane, from his bedroom window, the face a circle of light in the darkness.

He saw the garage door open and two tiny figures move through it. They came to the prone figure and bent over it, obscuring the face from view.

Low felt as if he were floating, that feeling of being in water. But he was sure he was not dreaming, this time. He looked up from the scene below and found Liang's face, glowing and solemn, bobbing about, as if he were on an invisible trampoline.

"Liang!" Low exclaimed. "Where've you come from?"

"Low...you were pulling me again..."

"But I thought..." Confused, Low looked downwards. "If you're up here with me, who is that down there?" He pointed. "I thought that was you!"

Liang's mouth stretched into a smile. "That's you, you fool. You fell. Like I did. Now we really are the same."

"I don't understand."

"I'll show you," said Liang.

"Liang..." he murmured. Liang swooped close to Low, setting him spinning. Dark and light swirled round him. He closed his eyes. He should have felt giddy but instead he felt as weightless as the air.

"Look," said Liang. "There I am!"

Low opened his eyes. The lane had vanished. Instead, a vast expanse of water stretched before his eyes, pewter grey and smooth in an early morning light.

"That's where I fell, see?" said Liang. Low saw a beach, shingled and starry from wetness, and a high cliff.

"We had to climb down there. And at night. For secrecy. We were halfway down when I fell. I can remember the pain of bouncing off the rocks as I went. But when I hit the bottom – pow! Nothing. Just this. It takes you a while to get used to being away from your body. There's mine, do you see? In that junk."

Low looked down at the grey sea. He could just make out a small boat with two masts, as grey as the sea itself. "But how can we be here...and somewhere else as well?" asked Low.

"I don't know. Anyway, I'm not going back."

"Why not?"

"I can't. I've tried. I can't get down."

"A silver cord..."

"What?"

"I'm not sure. Something I remember. About a cord – when you dream..."

"We aren't dreaming!"

"Then what are we doing?"

"Going to a new place. I've seen it. All white. No, not even white. There's no whiteness like it. It's a place of...of..."

"Well?"

Liang's voice sank. "Of ancestors," he whispered.

"No!" yelled Low. "That's not right! Not until you..."

"It's so lovely," came Liang's hushed tones. "Like sweetmeats and feeling warm and so happy you could just laugh for ever. Better than anything. Why go back?"

"Because..." Low began, looking down, trying to distinguish the figures that huddled in the stern of the junk. It's a strange boat, he thought. He looked up suddenly. Liang was swirling away from him. His face was a tiny glow and his voice distant.

"So lovely. Better than anything. Come with me, Low!"

Low felt the pull on him. His mind filled up with a great cry of "No!" and he thrust himself away from Liang's disappearing form. The sea beneath him moved in an arc and the spinning began again.

Not there, thought Low from within his vortex. Not towards the light. Not towards ancestors, the dead of a thousand years. No!

CHAPTER SIXTEEN

He saw first the cloudy grey sky of a new dawn. The sight of that sky, solidly above him, and the sensation of hard board beneath his back was so reassuring that he let out a half-gasp of relief from between his teeth. He was away from the vortex, and he had not gone with Liang towards the light.

"My son!"

The voice had the same sharp, accented strangeness as Liang's, but was deeper. The voice of a man. A face bent over him, a smile forming.

"My son has recovered! He is awake!"

The cry brought more faces, bending, looking down with interest.

"Ah, the boy is better."

"Just as well, the tide is ready for our departure."

"Raise the sails!"

"Let him sip this tea."

A scalding, sour liquid trickled on to his tongue. He spat and coughed, but the taste cleared his mind. "Liang..."

"He speaks his name – he is well!" The first man grasped him by one hand, squeezing it tightly. "Liang, my son! We thought you were lost to us."

"No...I'm not Liang...he went towards the light...something pulling...I can't remember." He put his hand over his eyes. The cloudless sky hurt his eyes and his head throbbed so badly he could hardly think. "Where am I?"

There was a muttering among the men.

"We cannot expect recovery all in a moment," said the man who was holding his hand. "A fall on the head can empty the mind of thoughts. Can you not recall, Liang, the climb down the steep cliff in darkness, last night? You lost your hold and—"

"Falling...spinning...I..." he tried to raise his head but it was too painful. "I was climbing up..."

"Down, down," said the men in unison. "We were all climbing down the cliff to the boat."

"Then you lost your grip and fell. Do you remember that?" asked the man who called himself Father.

He only had a vague recollection. He was balancing high above the ground, sailing out into the air, his foot caught in something. He heard the awful scream of a woman. But the images were so fuzzy he could not catch them properly – they were like soap bubbles, bursting before he could take a proper look.

"I...I was falling...then I nearly went into the light...Liang..." He closed his eyes from pain and sadness.

"He knows his own name. That is a good start," said an old man with a creaky voice.

"Not Liang..." it was a struggle to reply. The memory of that hazy time was slipping as fast as a dream after waking. And there was nothing to replace it. He didn't know where he was, or where he'd come from. He wasn't even sure *who* he was. If he wasn't Liang, as the men were telling him, who was he? No other name came to him, no memories before the place of the vortex. His mind was like a vacuum. "Liang is gone...into the light...the place...of ancestors..."

"No!" exclaimed the men. "Liang is here with us; badly hurt, but alive, praise the gods!"

"I...can't remember..." he admitted.

The junk creaking as though its wooden joints were in pain...the sailcloth clapping loudly as the wind hit it between the bamboo slats...another mouthful of moss-coloured tea...the motion of the vessel against the waves...the raw smell of the men...the ice-breath of the wind as they sailed. These were the only impressions the boy held in his thoughts.

The men waited, muttering. He looked from one face to the other. He was sure they were complete strangers to him, but he recognized them as his people, men he did not feel uncomfortable with. They seemed so sure of what they were saying, and the pain in his head prevented him from thinking clearly.

"Then, I am Liang?" he asked, at last. It was the only name he could recall, but it didn't seem to fit.

"What a question! Of course! You are my only son!" The man smiled, almost chuckled, but a feeling of sadness overwhelmed the boy. He could not smile back.

He struggled to sit up. An agony of pain, blotting out all other sensations, flooded into his left arm. "Oooeeewaagch!"

"Lie back, lie back," instructed his father. "You damaged your arm badly in the fall. Your upper arm and the back of your head. We have dressed them." His grin broadened. "Spare sailcloth makes good bandage. I will fetch you some opium to deaden the pain."

As he turned to move off, a black snake of heavy silk dragged against the boy's cheek. His father's hair was tied into a tight plait that hung down his back. He lifted his good arm to the nape of his neck. His fist grasped a similar coil.

Pigtail? he thought. Pigtail? The word sounded familiar, yet the fat braid felt alien, and nothing in his voided memory could tell him why.

CHAPTER SEVENTEEN

As the sun rose, saffron yellow and already burning hot, a wind caught the sails of the junk and took it fast on its course. The cliffs disappeared below the sea's horizon and the boat became a precarious haven in an endless water.

"The Sea of Nanyang is indeed vast," said the old man with the creaky voice, who was standing in the stern close to where Liang lay.

"Is that what we're sailing on, the Nanyang?" asked Liang, clenching his teeth against the waves of pain.

"The sea that stretches between us and our fortunes," the man said. "Behind us lies Kwantung. Before us the Isles of Nanyang!"

"We have come from...Kwantung, and we're going to...Nanyang," Liang repeated slowly, hoping that the words would mean something.

The old man grinned, showing his raw gums. "All my life I have dreamed of crossing this water." He shaded his eyes and looked ahead, as if he already saw land in the distance. "Ever since I was small I have heard of the fortunes men make on the Distant Isles of Nanyang."

"Is it very far, to these Distant Isles?" Liang was fascinated by the man's hair, which on account of his great age was nearly lost. Only a few strands remained, at the very back of his head. These he grew as long as any other man's, and he had twisted them, as best he could, into a skimpy pigtail.

"It is forty days' journey," said the man. He squatted down by the boy, in readiness for a long conversation. "They told me not to come, you know. All my family said I was far too old to start a new life. But I have come with my son, and his son. Since I was a lad I have watched the junks go down the river delta, to the sea, bound for foreign lands. All that time I longed to sail with them."

"Why?" Liang asked.

"You must know what it's like, farming the land around the Four Towns. Your father's land is not far from mine. Famine, most years. And when, finally, we manage to grow a little extra rice, the Emperor raises his taxes. Bah!" He gave a cackle. "We can say that freely now we've left his clutches. *Bah* to the Emperor!"

"The Four Towns," Liang repeated. "What are they?" He was desperate to find some clues that might nudge his memory back into place.

"Si Lap, the four towns round the delta of the Xijaing River."

"West river," repeated Liang. "West of where, honourable old sir?"

"Why, west of Kwantung, of course."

"Kwantung...why yes, Canton, of course!" sang Liang. At last a name that meant something. Just a niggle at the back of his mind, admittedly, but it made him feel elated, despite his aching arm and head. The word Canton summoned up all kinds of reassuring sensations, not memories exactly, but a feeling of belonging.

"Yes, Kwantung," said the old man, spitting over the side of the boat. "Sucker of men's blood. Of men's right to scratch a living from their soil. A jail without bars. I am glad to have left it."

"Why didn't you go before?" asked the boy.

The man gave him a strange look. "You should know why, as well as anyone. It is a punishable offence to leave the Emperor's domains. Punishable by death."

"You aren't allowed to leave Canton?" Liang repeated.

"Or any other province. But it's worse for us in the south. We can smell the sea. It makes the longing stronger."

"We shouldn't have left," said Liang, suddenly. "We'll all regret it."

"Why do you say that?" snapped the man. "What do you know about it?"

Liang closed his eyes. Why had he said such a thing to the venerable old man? He had insulted him, he knew that.

"You lost your mind," muttered the man. "With that fall down the cliff. You left half your brain on the shingle. Never thought you'd survive. Even your father thought he'd lost you...and here he is, Yap Ah Loy...greetings."

His father was bending over him again. In his hand he held an earthenware jug from which came a long piece of tubing. Inside the jug something hot smoked away.

"Take some, my son," said Yap. "To deaden the pain."

"What...is this?" asked Liang.

Yap started, as though surprised. "You have seen hookahs before," he said. He offered Liang the small mouthpiece that was at the end of the tubing. "Take. Smoke. Dream."

When Liang sucked the strange smoke into his lungs his thoughts swirled away from the boat that drifted on the sea. At first he felt calm. Then the impressions began, filling his mind with a myriad of smells, sounds and images.

But in his hookah dreams, he was not Liang, a poor farmer's son from Si Yap, west of Canton. Faces echoed from another place and time. Kitty's laughing brown eyes, Skiff's sharp nose, distorted by water, Wye Liew's grim mouth, Sau's gentle smile. Grey buildings, straight up into a grey sky.

Inside his opium haze, images formed, collapsed, formed again. Each one hinted at something once known, but now almost completely obliterated. When he opened his eyes again, the faces slipped away. But one last feeling, a sort of intuition, remained. Liang could remember nothing, but he knew that there was something he'd forgotten.

Is this what it's like for a new-born, he asked

himself? No past, just emptiness filled only with the absolute present? He saw clearly just how important memories were. I've lost my life, he thought. It's all gone in a fall from a cliff, everything that made me a person.

"You slept well?"

"Yes, Father." He yawned, drawing deep breaths of pure, sea air into tainted lungs. His mouth tasted of the dead. "How long have I been asleep?"

"A whole day. Through all of yesterday, our first day out into the sea, through the night, and now the sun is high above us again."

"I'm thirsty."

"You can drink. All your ration of water has been saved."

As Liang swallowed a bowl of water and some rice, his father watched him carefully. "Your mind is clearer, now?"

"A little," said Liang. "I'd like to get up, I think, try going for a walk." He was desperate to evade his father's questions.

Slowly, he picked himself off the deck. For a moment he swayed, then gained his footing. He moved along the side of the junk, hugging his bad arm to himself, stepping over people as he went.

The boat was crammed with life. People, almost all Chinese peasant farmers, sat or lay, their bodies squashed together, their bundles between their legs or under their heads, from the stern to the bow.

He realized that he had been given a lot more room than anyone else, a space to recover in...or to die in.

"Forty days, like this?" he asked himself, as he stumbled over a pair of legs.

"Hey, careful!"

"I'm sorry. I'm not used to the motion of the sea."

"You're Liang Ah Loy, aren't you?"

The speaker was a boy of thirteen or fourteen. He moved, as best he could, into an even smaller space, and motioned Liang to squat down beside him.

"You're the one that fell from the cliff, aren't you?" the boy continued, adding, "I'm Sam. Sam Ah Ho." He bent round and peered at the back of Liang's head. "You did yourself a lot of damage, I think."

Liang nodded, gingerly. "I can't remember things."

"What things?"

"Anything at all. Not my family or anything." His words were coloured with fear. "I don't even recognize my father."

"Oh, he's your father, all right. I saw you together on the way here. Besides, I've heard of this before. Someone in our district, an old man, fell from his horse and hit his head. His memory went, like yours. But it came back in the end, they say."

"It's awful," Liang confided. "I don't even know

why we're going to the Isles of Nanyang."

"To escape the famine," said Sam. "To work the mines – tin – that's what they mine. They say that you get plenty to eat, after each shift. I won't mind working, so long as there's food. I'm sick of feeling starved all the time. Stories come back from the Distant Isles about people becoming rich from mining tin, setting up their own businesses, living in luxury. My father plans to split our earnings into two; save half and send the rest to my mother. Then, when we've made enough profit, we'll buy our own tin mine and send for the women. It won't be long before we are a family again, if we all work hard!"

"What is tin?" asked Liang. "What's it used for?"

"It's a metal. It comes from the ground. I don't know what they do with it, but it's very precious."

"Like gold?"

"You remember some things, then."

Liang said, "It's only myself that's all a blank. My past, my history."

Sam roared with laughter. "Lucky you! I would like a bang on the head if it made me forget all the hunger, all the beatings, all the standing in the wet paddy fields day after day! *And* all the fighting."

"Fighting?"

"Take our family, for instance. We had a dispute with the See family. They paid less rent than us, yet my father could not see why. When we complained to the landowners, the Sees came in the night. They set our pigpen on fire. All the piglets were killed in the smoke, and the sow ran away – or was taken. So my father and my two elder brothers went to the Sees' land the following night. They were set upon by the Sees. They'd lain in wait. One of my brothers was killed in the fight." Sam's face contorted as he tried to control the onset of tears.

"That's horrible!"

"Yes," spat Sam. "Better to work all day in a tin mine than go on enduring that. My father said that when he was a boy, a feud like that ended in a whole village being burnt to the ground." Sam was quiet for a minute.

"Then," he went on, "after the last full moon, word went round about another sailing to the Distant Isles. We sent the women to my grandmother's cottage and walked to the coast. That's when I first saw you. But you can't remember me, is that right?"

Liang nodded. "I'm sorry that I can't." Chatting to Sam had helped ease the dreadful throbbing in his head and arm. Listening to Sam's stories had made him realize he was not the only unfortunate boy on the junk.

"Perhaps you would like to bring your rice portion up here to eat? It's nearly time."

"I'm not at all hungry. I think I'll miss my next portion."

Sam's eyes flew open. "Don't do that! The cooks will only share it out amongst themselves. Bring it up here, I'm starving! If you give me your food today, I'll be sure to return the favour, don't you fear!"

He gave Liang a gentle push. "Let's get in the queue nice and early. That's the way to get generous rations. Oh yes, I've worked it all out. I look after myself first. That's the only way to survive!"

With a cheery chuckle, he linked his arm through Liang's good one, and together they shuffled towards the galley.

CHAPTER EIGHTEEN

The five white pebbles rolled on to the deck.

"OK!" said Sam. "Your go!"

Liang arranged them neatly. He balanced one pebble on the back of his left hand and held his arm ready. He always used his bad arm for five-stones because he wanted it to grow strong again. Even now, almost six weeks after the fall, his grasp was weak and the muscles ached, sometimes very badly.

He threw the first stone, picked up a second and caught the first again.

"Bravo!" laughed Sam.

Liang poised himself again. As he did so, he became aware of a muttering. It seemed to go round the decks of the junk like a rice bowl being passed along a line. He and Sam looked up. Men were pointing, leaning out, their hands grasping the rails.

"Land!" The mutter became a whisper, the whisper a cry, the cry a shout.

"Land!"

"Land in the distance!"

Men dropped on to their knees. They lowered their heads and kissed the rough wood of the decks.

"Merciful ancestors, we have arrived!"

Sam and Liang looked at each other. The long journey was almost over. The stones were forgotten. They rushed to the bow of the boat, which was already crowded with passengers.

"Let us through!" Sam demanded. "We're too short to see over heads." He pushed and elbowed his way forward, with Liang keeping close in his wake. Finally they were at the front.

Sam looked at Liang with disappointment in his eyes. "I can't see anything."

The sun beat down on them and they replaced the pillbox caps which had been jostled off their heads by the crowd. Shading his eyes with a hand, Liang could just make out a grey line that rose from the sea, far off on the horizon.

"There!" he yelled, although his friend was right next to him. "Look! Land!"

It took over an hour for the grey, shapeless blob to become formed and green. Liang and Sam stood motionless as the new country loomed up before them. It was as though it were rising up out of the sea, Sam said. They had grown used to the flat infinity of water. This land, so solid, so huge, overawed them.

Sam found his arm being gripped tightly by his friend's good hand. He turned to find the most peculiar expression on Liang's face.

"I know this place." Excitement trilled in his voice.

"What?" Sam simply laughed. "Don't be a dunce. That's impossible."

Liang shook his head violently, although he knew this always brought on a headache. "I know this place," he repeated. "I just feel it...inside."

"I thought you couldn't remember things," said Sam, trying to catch him out.

"I remember this."

Sam got angry. "Listen. None of us have ever been here before. Don't be stupid! These are the Distant Islands. I don't care what you can or can't remember. You've never been here before."

"Nanyang, the Distant Islands," whispered Liang to himself. But the name meant nothing to him. He couldn't explain the feeling that was welling inside him. But he knew, with such certainty it hurt, that the weird, tangled shapes formed by the mangrove roots, the drooping fronds at the tops of the coconut palms, even the smell of the little cove they were sliding into were somehow part of his forgotten past.

They dropped anchor some way out, and a few of the crew waded ashore.

A group of Chinese men waited on the beach.

Each man was dressed in the same shabby blue coat and trousers as the boat passengers, with the addition of a wide-brimmed coolie hat. But one man, who stood well back from the muddy water-line, wore pale coloured silks and a neat satin pillbox cap. Even from the junk, Liang could see his beautiful embroidered slippers which turned up slightly at their pointed toes.

"That man is their leader," he told Sam.

"I hope they've brought us some food," said Sam. "I'm sick of nothing but noodles and rice. Even the tea's tasted odd, in the last week or so. Like the water's gone off. I can't wait for a bowl of fresh tea."

"Why do they carry all that rope?" asked Liang.

"Maybe the crew will tie it to the boat and pull us further in," Sam suggested. "I'm not keen on getting my feet wet. It reminds me of paddy fields!"

But the men did not return to the boat. After speaking with the welcoming party, they waved their arms at the junk.

The rest of the crew began to move about the deck. They shouted and pushed at people.

"Come on, get ashore," they snarled. Working in pairs, they heaved their passengers over the side of the boat into the water almost before they had time to gather up their bundles.

"Don't let's wait to be pushed in," urged Liang. When people jostled him, his arm and head always hurt.

Sam made a face. "Doesn't look like we've got a choice," he sighed. "Let's go."

He hurled himself off the deck feet first. Liang watched for a second or two. Then he jumped. His bare feet and legs hit cold water. He staggered, pulled himself upright and looked back towards the junk just in time to see his father leap down, their fat bundle held high in his arms.

Everyone waded ashore.

"Perhaps we'll get fish, or even meat," said Sam, as he sloshed through the water. "I've longed for meat ever since the supply ran out. What do you want the most?"

"A hookah," said Liang shortly. He was rather worried about his longing for the nightly opium. Sometimes, towards the time his father brought him the smoking pot, his body would begin to shake like leaves in a breeze. It seemed to know it was nearly time. Most of the dreams he had under the influence of the drug vanished as he woke, but the feelings they left made him long straight away for the next pipe. He could have lived for ever inside those elusive dreams, so warm and enticing were their fragrance and flavour.

As the passengers reached the shore, they were herded into a group by the men in coolie hats and made to sit, cross-legged, on the mud between the roots of the mangrove trees. Liang, slower on his feet than Sam, was grabbed by his bad arm and pulled into place. He let out a yelp of pain.

"Kindly let go of my friend, honourable sir," said Sam, in the formal way needed even for rough, unpleasant strangers. "He has had an accident."

"That so?" said the man, with no formality at all. He took hold of Sam by his pigtail and swung him down on to the mud, before walking away.

"This is no welcoming party," growled Sam.

The mud had a bad smell and its surface was a mass of long, thin worms that wriggled without stopping, so that it seemed as if the whole beach were moving. The two boys watched as the shore party and the crew bargained hotly over something. Money changed hands. The captain of the trading junk pocketed a bag of glinting coins, signalled to his crew and began to wade back towards the vessel.

The anchor was dragged into the boat and its sails filled as the oarsmen turned it into the wind. Liang spotted one of the watching eyes painted on the bow as the junk moved out into the open sea. They were there to watch out for evil spirits, but to Liang it seemed that the boat itself observed their predicament as it left them behind.

For a moment, things were silent and still, as everyone watched the boat depart. Then the man with the embroidered slippers began to speak in high, rapid Cantonese.

"Welcome to Nanyang. My name is Leong Po Hang, and I am your Towkay. I own several tin mines, and I am looking for workers. You are very lucky. There is work for all of you at one mine. It is newly opened and not far from here. Only one day's march inland. You will follow us, please."

He turned away. Several of the men from the junk jumped up and began shouting.

"Hang on a minute," said one. "We want to see the lie of the land before we choose where we work. And we want to know the wage we're being offered. And we're all tired, and very hungry. We want a meal, before we go anywhere."

Everyone, Sam and Liang included, began yelling and waving in agreement with this.

The Towkay spoke in whispers to his men. The yelling died down, expectantly.

Po Hang gave a few sharp words of command. His men pulled little pointed daggers from their belts. The knives flashed and threatened. Within minutes the bedraggled travellers were formed into a long line, with each man's pigtail fastened to the coil of rope. Sam was behind Liang in this human chain. Liang's father was further down the line, his face dark and furious. Suddenly he cried out, waving his fist above his head.

"Tricksters! Cheats! When we set out we were promised riches! You have turned us into slaves!"

But the men with the knives only laughed, and jerked the rope cruelly, so that Yap Ah Loy stumbled.

Po Hang tied both ends of the rope round two of his men's waists and the line of prisoners moved slowly forward, out of the stinking swamps and towards the far-off hills.

CHAPTER NINETEEN

BONG! BONG! BONG! BONG...

Liang cracked open his eyes and peered out from beneath the fringe of his lashes.

New morning light, diffuse and edged with grey, filtered into the sleeping hut through the wide cracks between the wooden slats. Almost brushing his face was Sam's dark pigtail. The two boys lay close together because there was no spare room to spread out. There were twenty other lads in the same small hut.

BONG! BONG! BONG! BONG...

At each vibrating strike of the gong, Liang's head throbbed with a pain that made his stomach churn. He put his hand to his eyes to shield them from the hostile light. His headaches had got much worse since they had come to the tin mine.

All round him, boys were rising from their sleep. They moved slowly and silently, numbed by thoughts of each day's ordeal.

They look like the tiny waves on a calm sea, thought Liang, as he watched from his sleeping mat. Bottoms and heads were rising and falling, rising and falling.

"Come on, Liang, get up, get up," said Sam, pushing him with the sole of his foot. "Or I'll go on without you."

Liang managed a grin. Even in this place of the damned, he thought, Sam could cheer him up. Sam was always first in the breakfast queue, even if it meant being allocated the worst job after breakfast.

Breakfast was half a coconut shell filled with cold rice. Liang dipped his fingers in and stuffed the rice into his mouth. It tasted rancid, as though it had been left for days to go off.

He took the emptied shell to the water barrel. He skimmed the green scum that floated on the top away with his hand and plunged the nut shell fast into the water and away again. This was the best way of getting a clearer drink, but the water tasted more foul than the rice and he dashed half of it into the ground.

For one or two minutes, no one yelled at him to begin work. He dallied by the water butt, watching Sam at his first chore of the day. He had a pile of sticks, ropes and baskets and a queue of men. Sam tied lengths of rope to two shallow baskets, slipped the loops over the ends of a carrying-stick, and handed it to a waiting miner. He was good at his jobs now. Even turning the huge water-wheel didn't seem to give him trouble. Two weeks, Liang reminded himself. Two weeks they had all been here, working for the Towkay in the tin mines of the Distant Islands of Nanyang.

The two weeks seemed equally no time at all and for ever.

They had arrived at the new mine with blisters,

sores and bruises. Leeches stuck tenaciously to their legs, sucking blood until they were as fat as ripe fruit.

They had been given a first coconut bowl of rice, some thin clothes, a coolie hat to shade them from the sun and a mat in a sleeping hut.

They had been sorted into groups – like farm cattle, the men grumbled – the old from the young, the weak from the strong. Sam's older brother, fully grown with muscles he proudly rippled for the overseers, was sent to work in the mine with the boys' fathers. Sam was set to running errands, fetching, carrying and repairing anything that was broken.

But Liang's arm still hung oddly – as though his elbow had been put on back to front, Sam said. It had little power in it and ached badly when it was cold. He was no good for heavy work. He found himself working alongside the old men. They knelt by the stream that ran through the site and washed buckets of muddy stones, swirling them in the water and picking out any tiny flecks of silvery tin.

Next to Liang worked the old man with the bald head and skinny pigtail whom he'd met on the junk. On their first day, he'd smiled at Liang and told him his name was Cheng.

"You were right," he'd said, as they sifted stones on their first day.

"I am sorry, honourable sir?" said Liang.

"You said, on the journey, that we should not have come. I wonder how you knew? Everyone else was so excited...so...*fooled.*"

"I said that?" asked Liang. His memories of the early part of their journey were as confused as hookah dreams.

At the end of that first long day, they had gathered less than a handful of tin.

"None of us will ever get rich if that is all the tin we can collect in one day," said Liang.

Cheng laughed. "But these are only the gleanings!" and seeing Liang's puzzled face went on to explain that the basketfuls of mined tin ore were sifted further up the stream by some of the more trusted workers, carefully overseen. The mud and stones the old men and Liang sifted through were the gleanings from that first sifting. At the end of the day, the tiny pile of tin was carefully weighed on a little spring scale.

"No one trusts anyone in this place," Cheng had said, under his breath.

Although being with the old men made him feel bitter about his arm, Liang liked working alongside Cheng, who chatted constantly about his past life. The tales of his childhood, youth and manhood made the days speed along more quickly.

But today, Liang had difficulty listening. His head ached so badly he wanted to dash it against the hard ground. In front of his eyes danced spots – black, pink, orange. Cheng's high-pitched gravel voice seemed to come from a long way off.

"Your head, it pains you?" Liang heard, through

the fuzz. He nodded.

"I cannot see the tin in the water," he confessed.

Cheng came up close to him.

"This evening, we will go to Langat together," he said. "When the other boys settle to sleep, leave your mat and meet me by my hut."

Liang didn't answer right away. The sun beat down as if it were determined to burn them all alive. He cupped his hands and scooped up stream water, drinking a gulp of it and splashing the rest over his face and neck. He knew what they would find in Langat village. There, the opium dealer kept late hours for the men from the mine.

"All right," he said. "I'll be there."

When the water-wheel finally slowed to a creaking halt at the end of the long day, Liang found himself next to Sam and his brother in the queue for food and tea.

"Come and join us," Sam urged.

They carried their rice and fish and the steaming bowls of longed-for tea into the shade behind the men's sleeping hut.

When they were settled, Sam's older brother, looking round first to see that they were not overheard, leant across to Liang.

"We are sick of this stinking hell-hole," he whispered.

Liang nodded in agreement. Everyone felt let down and angry at the way they'd been tricked. Sam's brother was angry, Liang could see. It was not the Chinese way to show anger, but gobs of spit shot from his lips as he spoke and his eyes shone with an inner fever.

"Have you heard of the Sultan of Langat?" asked Sam. "He rules this part of the island. There is a rumour going round the camp. Men say he does not like the Chinese tin mines."

Liang began swallowing the fish and rice. His stomach was so empty by this time of the day that even the stale food tasted heavenly.

"They say," Sam went on, "that poor miners who go to him and ask for mercy and a fairer deal are given enough money to pay for their passage home."

Liang choked on his food. "But – we cannot go home," he stammered. "Everyone says so. No one is allowed to leave the Emperor's domains. Those who return are put to death."

"Only if they are caught," Sam's brother whispered. "We would dive off the boat before we reached Kwantung and swim ashore."

"But why should he help us, if he doesn't like the Chinese?" asked Liang.

"The mines take riches away from his coffers," said Sam's brother. "And he would like to see the back of them. So he helps those who would go home. Without workers, the mines would fail."

"At least, that is what people say," said Sam. "We're going to try our luck with him." He looked at Liang.

"Will you come with us to ask the Sultan?"

Liang looked down at his arm. "I couldn't swim very far with this," he said, shortly.

Sam's brother got to his feet. "Before anything else, we must ask our father. And you should consult yours, Liang. They are the ones who must make the final choice."

Sam and Liang bowed their heads before such wise words. Of course, thought Liang, our duty is to our fathers. Whatever they say...

As the luminous twilight began to darken, Sam and Liang stretched out on their sleeping mats. Sam took his friend's good arm and squeezed it tightly.

"Dream sweetly, brother," he whispered. "Dream of home." He rolled over, and like all the exhausted boys in the hut, fell almost instantly asleep.

Liang closed his eyes, but his head and arm throbbed so badly it was impossible for him to drift off to sleep quickly.

"...*This evening, we will go to Langat together...*"

Liang's eyes opened wide as he remembered the old man's words. He longed for the deadening sleep that a hookah brought. Silently he rose from his mat and crept between the rows of sighing, snoring bodies into the darkness of the Malay night.

CHAPTER TWENTY

The opium peddler filled long bamboo pipes with the dried sap of poppy seeds. He sat cross-legged in his dilapidated little wooden hut, and crooned tunelessly as he worked.

Liang and Cheng crouched on the mud floor in front of him. There were ten or so miners in the hut. Some already had their hookahs and were lying in the darkness at the very back. The others crushed in on the peddler, anxious to be next, their dry tongues licking their dry mouths.

Liang watched the peddler hold a bamboo pipe over the flame of a small oil lamp. He had skewered it on to a length of steel so that he didn't burn his fingers. As the opium toasted, an aroma rose into the air, and the noses of the waiting miners rose with it.

He handed the pipe to Liang. "The young before the old," he cackled. Liang handed him the money he had received from the overseers. All his meagre wages were going on dreams of oblivion.

Liang took his hookah over to a dark corner where men were smoking, talking and drinking hot tea. At intervals, a burst of laughter would drown the crooning voice of the opium peddler. Soon, Cheng had joined him. He brought with him a coconut, still full of moist white flesh, and offered a half-shell to Liang.

Liang lay with his back against the wall of the hut. He chewed the sweet nut, sipped piping hot tea and smoked his pipe. The chatter of the men swelled over him until it joined with the noises of the night outside: the owl's hoot, the nightjar's shrill call. He closed his eyes. This was the closest he had come to feeling peaceful since they'd landed.

As his mind wandered, Liang thought of Sam and his brother's plan. Well, he thought, who doesn't want to get away from this place? But Liang hadn't sought out his father to ask him. He'd meant to, but something kept getting in the way. His father was still a stranger to him and Liang found it hard to begin a conversation with him.

But it wasn't just that, he now realized. His father might be enthusiastic about the plan. He might jump at the chance to see the old country again. But the old country meant nothing to Liang. He'd been told about the mother and the two sisters he'd left behind in Kwantung, but they meant less to him than the characters from a story told over bowls of tea.

As the opium took over and Liang slid away from the hut into the freedom of dreams, he saw clearly why he was reluctant to go back to Kwantung. From the moment they had sailed into the bay, he'd felt he belonged *here*. The smell, the noises, the look of the place seemed familiar to him.

If only I could get away from this terrible mine, he thought, I might find out why the place feels so familiar.

Maybe he could run off into the forest with the Ho family, when they left the mine, then look for a settlement that would be kind enough to take in a crippled boy with no past.

"That's a pipe dream, Liang," he told himself, and chuckled quietly at his unintentional joke as he sucked at the pipe and prepared to dream.

They say that when you're starving, your dreams are filled with food.

He was sitting on the step of a doorway that seemed too tall and too wide. He stuffed sugary sweetmeats into his mouth.

I'm smaller, he thought, luxuriating in the sweet taste. A little child of five or six.

Suddenly, the door was no longer at his back. He was walking along a hardbaked dirt track. He looked down at himself. He had grown, but his clothes were the opposite of his usual – bare legs and arms – but his feet were covered by brightly-coloured footwear. Instinctively, he knew that years had passed since he chewed the sweetmeats.

Under the garment that covered his chest something warm and furry wriggled. He was holding it very carefully, below the cloth.

As he walked between the tall trees he was approached by a skinny, sneak-eyed man wearing a faded pink and yellow cotton wrap.

"What have you got there?" asked the man, mopping his face with a dirty scrap of towelling.

"A squirrel," said the boy. The answer surprised him, because a moment before he had not known what he was cradling.

The man peered down the tee-shirt at the animal. "A flying squirrel," he agreed, "and not fully grown. Where did you get it?"

Liang chose to ignore this question. He walked on. Trees were all around them now, their tops touching the clouds. Lemon sunlight made the leaves sparkle like diamonds.

"I'll give you a pack of Cokes for it," said the man. "Twelve cans."

The boy smiled. He shook his head. He lifted the creature out and gently examined the soft webbed skin that stretched between back and front paws. He knew why he was walking into the forest. The squirrel lived there.

"I'll give you five good dollars," said the man. "Malaysian ringgits."

"No," Liang replied. He felt the squirrel was somehow threatened by the man.

"Ten!" The man increased his offer with a sort of squawk, and wiped more sweat from his face.

In answer, the boy put the squirrel on the thick, green forest floor. Without even the pretence of a goodbye, the squirrel scurried away and shinned up the nearest trunk. Almost immediately, it was flying a great distance through the air, its webbed legs stretched full out.

"Wow! He looks like a kite!" He turned to the

man to share his joy at the animal's freedom. The man no longer wore the grubby cotton wrap. He was dressed in a dark suit of clothes with a white shirt. His smile showed a glint of gold.

The word "father" settled into the twists and turns of Liang's dreaming mind.

When he turned to catch one more glance of the squirrel, the forest had gone. The creature that flew in the clear air was shining silver, huge and noisy.

"The planes are even bigger than I imagined, Father."

"Big and fast, my son," said the man. "It is time to board."

Liang felt those colourful shoes root him to the ground. "I...I don't want to go," he said. "This is where I belong."

"Come on," snapped the man. He grabbed his arm and pulled sharply.

"YEEYEOUW!" Liang cried out. It was his bad arm that was being pulled, and the pain was more real than the taste of the sweetmeat.

"Come on, boy, get up!" The fog of drugged dreams had only half lifted. The face close to Liang's could have been any man's, the father with the loose blue coolie trousers or the father with the smart grey suit, the man with the pink wrap or an overseer from the mines.

"Up, I say, you speck of scum!"

The mists lifted slightly and Liang knew it was the face of an overseer.

"Your sweet dreams are over – for good!"

Liang blinked and blinked again. He felt a pull on his scalp which made him struggle to his bare feet. The overseer was tying his pigtail to a length of rope.

Captive again, he thought, as he and the overseer moved through the throng of still–snoring men, past the opium peddler's oil lamp, now spent and black with charcoal from the night's work.

Outside, the sun had long been up. They crossed the stream by a rickety bamboo bridge. A heat haze made everything shimmer: the bridge, the storage sheds ahead, the creepers that tied themselves to the trunks of the trees. Liang looked up into the treetops and saw how they glinted like tin in a muddy stream.

In the flash of a split second, the dream flew into his mind. He marvelled at it all, from the taste of sweets to the pain in his arm.

I mustn't forget, he thought. He had no idea why it should be important, but he squeezed his eyes shut to help the pictures imprint themselves on to his thoughts.

All memories are important, he thought, when you haven't got many. But what was "Coke"? Or "planes"? And why did his father have such a different face? He recalled the glint of gold in the man's mouth. His father was too poor a farmer to have gold teeth. Perhaps, in his dream, he'd got his father muddled with the Towkay, Leong Po Hang, whose mouth was full of gold.

He hurried forward, trying to catch up with the overseer.

"I'm truly sorry, honourable sir," Liang began. "I did not mean to oversleep. I will work longer this evening—"

He stopped short as the man barked out a short laugh.

"Work longer!" he said. "And will you do the work of four men for me?"

Liang shook his head in confusion.

"You're in a lot of trouble, Lame-Arm," snapped the overseer, with a look of mocking delight. "You're the only one we've found yet, so your honourable Towkay is going to have the pleasure of taking all his wrath out on you."

Chapter Twenty-One

The Towkay-shed was Leong Po Hang's office. Its raised floor kept the dampness out and Liang's bare soles sank into soft carpet. For a second or two he luxuriated in the warm, tickling sensation, then he realized that Po Hang was staring at him and he dropped to his knees and rested the top of his head on the carpet pile.

"A thousand apologies, most honourable sir, for my laziness and lateness today," he muttered.

"Be quiet," said Po Hang.

"That's right, shut up," said the overseer.

Liang felt a pain in his ribs which toppled him over. The overseer had kicked him. He scrabbled back into a kneeling position.

"You didn't get very far," said Hang, walking slowly towards Liang. "Did you?"

Liang raised his head a little, so that he could see Hang through his lashes. He had no idea what the Towkay meant.

"Lazy is right," added the overseer with a coarse laugh. "He can't even run away without hitting the first opium den!"

"I wasn't running away," said Liang quickly. "Honourable sir, I had no intention of that. I took too much opium and failed to hear the gong. A thousand apologies—"

"Stop those lies!" For the first time, Hang raised his voice a little, but he was still not shouting. "Your friends have got a little further than you. They did not stop for a smoke. I want to know where you were all heading. Where are they now?"

The sharpness in his tone made Liang's head spin.

"I...what...which friends?" he managed at last.

The overseer's cloth slipper punched at his ribs again.

"Lim Ah Ah, Yap Ah Ho and Sam Ah Ho!" the overseer yelled. "All disappeared with you last night. One complete family, two strong workers and one nimble boy. You were the only dud among them. Just our luck to get only you back!"

Liang's mouth slackened in surprise. "Sam? Gone?" was all he could manage.

"All the Ho family," said Po Hang. "And you. So now you're going to tell us where they were heading."

Liang dropped his head again. He looked at the intricate patterns in the carpet. His thoughts raced. He shook his head like a dog to clear his thoughts.

"Why do you shake, boy? Speak!"

This time the overseer's foot attacked Liang's back and he sprawled forward on to his front at the impact.

"That is better! Stay like that!" laughed the man.

"Get him outside," said Po Hang. "He's ruining my carpet."

The overseer took Liang by the thickness of his

pigtail and swung him towards the door of the Towkay-shed. Outside, Liang was dropped into the dry dust, where he sprawled, the taste of earth in his mouth.

"Tell me about the escape," said Po Hang, quietly. He walked down the steps from his office until he stood over Liang. "My men know many tricks with their feet, with their fists and with their whips. So tell me now."

Liang shook his head furiously. "I know nothing. Please, believe me. I was never with them. I was with Cheng, the old man who washes gleanings with me. He was the one who took me to the opium den. Ask him!"

For a moment or two, both men were silent. Liang watched them exchange silent glances.

"It is well known that Sam Ah Ho was your particular friend," said Hang.

"We were friends. But he said nothing to me about leaving."

Leong Po Hang gave a slight nod. Just the smallest of actions, a tiny bob of the head, but it was enough. The overseer came at Liang, fists tight. He attacked his head, shoulders and then concentrated on Liang's bad arm. When Liang rolled into a ball to protect himself, the overseer used his whip.

"I tell the truth!" Liang screamed. "Honourable sirs! Believe me! I tell the truth! Ask the old man!"

He felt the searing slashes of the overseer's whip lash down on his back. He whimpered now, not daring to move from the rounded shape he'd curled into.

Finally the onslaught ceased, and Liang was allowed to crawl into the coolness below the raised floor of the hut. They left him there while they went to find Cheng.

Liang was surprised that he'd shed no tears. The beating had left him feeling weak and aching. His back stung, and down his arm shot waves of pain, but he did not feel in the least unhappy.

He had not told. Sam's secret had been kept safe. The only thing that made him sorrowful was that Sam had not had a chance to say goodbye. He imagined him, waking up in the dead of night, called by his father to leave straight away, and finding Liang's sleeping space already empty. He hoped that Sam would reach the Sultan's palace.

Slowly he stretched his limbs and tried each of them out. He raised himself to his feet, leant against the wall of the shed and massaged his arm. The elbow felt spongy and swollen.

He saw Leong Po Hang and the overseer walking towards him from the other side of the site. They spoke in low voices. Liang's knees gave way at the thought of another beating.

"No," he whispered to himself. It was cruel, the way the man had attacked his arm. He knew if it happened again, he would tell them about the Sultan of Langat. The thought made his empty stomach churn and he sank into the dirt as green bile rose into his mouth.

"Get up, puky weakling," said the overseer. "The Towkay wants to speak to you."

Wet with vomit, Liang scrambled to his feet. Leong Po Hang, mindful of his slippers, maintained his distance. "We will not worry ourselves further with the Ho family," he said. "The forest is full of many dangers. No doubt they are tiger-meat by now. I am more concerned about the loss of two fine miners. You will take their place, boy. You can start in the mine this very moment."

Liang could hardly believe his ears. Instead of punishment, they were giving him the plum job. Miners were supposed to take a higher percentage of the profit, and they were looked up to by all the other workers.

"Thank you, honourable sir!" he cried, bowing low.

"But wash that sick off first," laughed the overseer. He seemed to find all this very funny. His laughter grew louder and louder. It followed Liang as he walked towards the water butt – mocking, ribald, humourless.

CHAPTER TWENTY-TWO

Liang soon discovered why the miners were considered highest in position. Their job was the hardest and most dangerous.

He stood at the edge of the mine shaft. Tears of pain, fear and despair welled in his eyes. A miner scurried past him, stepped on to the ladder and disappeared from view. Liang wiped his face with the dirty palm of his hand.

"I'm a miner now," he told himself. "And miners are strong and brave. They do not sob like toddlers."

The throbbing in his head had redoubled in intensity. His back stung from the whipping and his left arm had lost all its power.

But worse than all the pains that plagued him were the after-effects of smoking the hookah the previous night. His mind was thick and heavy, and only half awake. Nothing seemed quite real. The world spun round him. The giddy feeling made him gag.

If only they'd given me time to recover, he thought. Just one good night's sleep and a meal might have made me feel stronger.

But he was in disgrace. There would be no time off for Liang. He balanced his shoulder-stick and climbed, for the first time, down into the tin mine.

The two ladders, for ascent and descent, were ingeniously carved from the tall trunks of forest trees. Each step was cut out of the wood. Some cuts were deep and straight, affording a good foothold, but other steps were badly carved and had been made slippery by the slime of the miner's muddy feet.

Liang climbed as slowly as he could, but the steps were used by all the miners and when some caught up with him he was heckled and threatened from above.

"Get a move on, littl'un!"

"Put a spurt in it, or I'll tread on your fingers!"

"By the ancestors, you're too puny a wretch to be down the mine!"

Liang almost slid the last ten metres, landing in a heap on the gritty mine floor, his baskets in a mess.

"Start on that pile over there," ordered the mine overseer.

Liang scooped the dug-out clay and pebbles into his baskets. He could see the tin glinting as he scooped. Riches, he thought, and as he did so the words of the Towkay came back to him, "Tell me about the escape."

Escape? thought Liang. It was a strange word for a boss to use. The meaning shot through him.

I'll never get away from this place, he thought. They come to find you, search you out in the jungle.

And now Sam is gone, what chance do I have?

"We are not free any more," he told himself. "They think of us as their slaves. We'll never get profits from this tin. They will work us until we die, then keep the profits for themselves."

He slung his shoulder-pole on, to his good side. The baskets swung and knocked at him, scratching his legs. He began the ascent, taking the tree-trunk ladder a step at a time. The bamboo pole dug deeply into his shoulder.

He was nearly at the top. The sun beat down on him in its midday strength, piercing Liang's head through with pain. Sweat dripped from his brow and stung his eyes, making it difficult for him to see.

He blinked several times, hanging on to the tree trunk ladder and not moving. It felt as though he was looking through water. Everything was swimming in front of his eyes. And then, as if it were giving up its struggle, his body started a violent trembling. He knew it was begging for more opium.

"A curse on hookah pipes," he muttered, trying to wipe the sweat off on to his collar. He wished he'd never breathed in the sickly poppy smoke.

The next step was narrow, badly carved and slimy with mud. He felt his footing slip and he clung to the trunk tightly with his good hand. But his foot slid off the step, knocking him off balance, and the pole and baskets rolled off his shoulder. The ropes tangled themselves round his good arm, dragging his hand away from its hold.

His body swayed outwards, his hands worked fruitlessly to gain a new grip.

He let out a wild, terrified cry. "AAAHHHH!"

Everyone paused in their work to watch the boy fall. So far, this was the third. One man had only broken his leg, but the other had died on the instant. The miners were getting used to it. When Liang landed with an unpleasantly final thud, only a few men walked over to peer at the body.

CHAPTER TWENTY-THREE

The light hurt his eyes, even through closed lids.

At first, as consciousness dragged his mind through the netted mists, he did not realize his eyes were shut. He realized nothing, except that there was pain, and light.

Then, all at once, sensations and images tore through his mind. A memory of falling – catapulting down, trying to save himself, scrabbling with hands, ears full of the sound of screaming.

"No." Involuntarily, his head moved, his eyelids squeezed tight. He must block out the light. He must not move towards it.

"He spoke – muttered something."

"Call his name."

"Low, oh Low, can you hear me?"

He brought his hands up, covered his eyes with his fingers and peered through. Blocking the light was the neat, almond-shaped face of his mother. Sau Kit whispered his name. Her hands reached round the back of his head, cradling it. She laid her cheek on his cheek, dampening his skin.

"My son...oh...we were so afraid...my son..." She kissed him, first one cheek then the other, then his forehead. She smoothed his hair.

It was like a fairground ride, shooting down,

down, until you are all stomach, then up again, fast, until you are all scalp. Up, down, up, down, the memories swung in on him, making their own noise, a sort of overwhelming whirring sound, shouts and cries buzzing in his head.

He filled his lungs with breath. This seemed to help. His thoughts sorted themselves into a better order. He could take them backwards, past the fall into the tin mine, past the journey on the junk, past the swirling time with Liang, to Tang's Take-Away. Past that to the time of his grandmother.

I must not forget, he promised himself. He knew memories could be elusive, they could slip away, leaving only a taste in the mouth.

Suddenly there were many voices. He opened his eyes properly and saw people in white coats coming towards him, pushing a piece of electrical equipment on wheels.

"He's all right now," came a woman's voice. "You can take that away again." And she laughed, a happy sound.

Low rolled his head towards her voice. He realized he was lying flat on a narrow bed in a room with white walls and too-bright strip-lighting above him.

"What...?" he muttered.

"Hello, Low." It was a young woman in a blue uniform. "You're probably wondering where you are. You're in the Casualty Department. We were all a bit worried about you for a moment or two.

You've had a nasty fall."

"I couldn't hold on to the ladder...it was the mud..."

"What did he say?" asked the nurse, turning to Low's parents.

"I'm not sure," said Wye Liew Tang, who was on the other side of the bed. He took Low's cold hand between both of his and squeezed it gently. "You fell from the fence, Low," said his father in Cantonese. "Don't you remember?"

"I fell from the fence," Low echoed. And then added, "My arm doesn't hurt!"

"You didn't hurt your arm," Sau pointed out. "But you've got a nasty gash on the side of your head."

Low shook his head, restlessly. He closed his eyes again. Confusion made his head spin again. He couldn't make sense of all the falls – from a cliff, from a fence, from a tree-trunk ladder..."It wasn't a fence," he mumbled. "I fell down a mine shaft, a great distance, down and down..."

His father gave a pleasant chuckle. "He has been dreaming," he told the nurse. "You relived your fall in a dream, my son," he told Low.

"Of course," said Low. He took another deliciously deep breath. "It must have been a dream." But how clear! How tangible! So vivid that it felt closer to him than reality.

One of the doctors was examining Low. Light shone into his eyes, making him blink. The doctor knocked at his knees with a little hammer. Cool fingers slipped over his wrist, searching out the pulse beat of his heart.

"It's rather odd," she said, finally, "but I'm pleased to say that I can't find much wrong. The knock on the head caused temporary concussion and respiratory distress but he's come round quite naturally and doesn't seem to have sustained any real harm.

"You'll have to stay in hospital for one night, old son," she added to Low. "Just in case. But we might let you go home tomorrow."

Low managed a smile. Of course – he was sure of where he was now. This was England and the strange language the doctor spoke was English. He remembered now. Her soft tones were soothing after the brassy cries of the Cantonese miners.

"She said..." began Wye Liew, ready to translate.

"I think I picked up a bit," said Low, slowly. "Something about hospital. Do I have to stay here?"

"You understood, you understood!" cried Sau in amazement. She took her son up into her arms and kissed and kissed him.

Low made a small pretence of being rather sickened and embarrassed by this display of emotion, but very soon he flung his own arms round her body and a feeling of delight coursed through him. One thing had not slipped his mind. Since he had lived at Tang's Take-Away, Sau had never kissed or hugged him until this moment.

CHAPTER TWENTY-FOUR

"Hello, Low," said the sun bird.

It was Sue Kung, resplendent in crimson pantaloons and an embroidered waistcoat.

Low grinned. "How did you know I was in hospital?"

"I had a message telling me not to go into school today, because you were here. So I thought I'd pop in to see what was wrong."

"Nothing much," said Low, making a face. "I fell off the back fence, that's all. I'm getting out this afternoon. My father is coming to pick me up. I can't wait."

Low had spent a sleepless night, partly because of the lights and buzzers and the hushed movements of the nurses but partly because he was frightened to go to sleep.

"I'm not going back there," he found himself whispering, each time his eyelids grew heavy. Would he be able to get himself back from Nanyang a second time?

When Low had told his parents about his strange experience, they had smiled and patted the back of his hand and told him that dreams could sometimes be most vivid. He wondered how Sue would react, if he told her. Would she believe him?

"Guess how long I was unconscious," he said, at

last.

"Well?"

"Fifteen minutes. Fifteen minutes! I can hardly believe that, but my mother and the doctor said it's true. I fell off the fence, my father phoned for an ambulance and they closed the shop down and came straight to the hospital. My mother said that they were so worried about my heart and my breathing that some special doctors were called. But I came round before they got to me." He gave a broad grin.

"You look almost happy about it," said Sue, puzzled.

"I was glad to be back."

"Back!"

"I can remember every moment that I was unconscious. But those memories didn't last for quarter of an hour. They lasted for ages. Months! When I came round I couldn't understand where I was for a while."

"What did you dream?" asked Sue.

"I think I was in Malaysia but it was called something different. It was called Nanyang."

"Nanyang," said Sue. "That sounds like a Chinese name."

"Well, I've never heard of it before."

"You must have!" Sue burst out with one of her laughs. "You certainly can't dream of things you've never heard of."

"Can't you?" asked Low, quietly. "Sue, I'm not sure that it *was* a dream. It was as if I was another boy. I felt *his* pains, *his* hunger. I lived his life and I can remember every moment of it."

"Go on then," said Sue, quietly. "Tell me."

It was a relief to talk about it again. But as he told Liang's story, he watched Sue's face become more and more disbelieving.

"I think you must have learnt all this – say, in a project in your other school – and then forgotten it," said Sue, doubtfully, as he finished. "Finally, it turned up in a dream. I've heard before that dreams are different when you've been knocked out."

Low looked down at the swirls on the faded pink bedspread. No one will ever believe me, he thought. If Sue doesn't, who would? I'll be better off not telling anyone at all. I'll only be laughed at.

"I just want to go home, really," he said at last.

"I know," said Sue. "I know you long to go back to Malaysia."

Low sat bolt upright in bed. "I meant Tang's Take-Away," he said. "Not Malaysia." It felt as if he *had* been back, thrown back into a nightmare Malaysia. He saw the cruel black eyes of the overseer again as he lay cowering at his feet...

"I'm not sure I want to go back to Malaysia any more," he said, a shudder passing through him.

Wye Liew Tang drove the car slowly along the back lane and manoeuvred it into his garage.

Low opened the passenger door and jumped out, determined to show his father that he was already feeling fit. He went into the lane.

"Is there a patch of blood where I fell off the fence?" he asked.

His father burst out in a great gusty laugh. Low looked up, half afraid. He'd never heard his father laugh as loud.

"Oh yes, a great pool of it, but your mother washed it away."

"Are you joking, Father?"

"You think I have no sense of humour, because I sometimes lose my temper," said Wye Liew. "But a man who can shout can also laugh, you know. Perhaps we should try to find the time to laugh together."

Low realized that this would be the closest his father would ever get to an apology. He risked a smile as he nodded, then looked away, unsure, down the lane.

This was the place he had first seen Liang. It seemed almost years ago. He supposed he would never see him again.

And yet...he was sure he heard a rustling in the bushes. His heart raced. He moved a few paces, his feet light on the tarmac.

Within the shadows of a slatted fence, something moved, very slightly. With a sudden leap, a figure jumped out into the lane.

"Ha-ya!"

Low sucked in his breath in terror. Another figure leapt out from the hiding place into a fighting stance, threatening, feet apart, hands flattened. "Ha-ya!"

"Stop it!" Low yelled at the top of his voice. White hot anger ripped off the lid of his fright. "Idiots! What are you playing at! Fools!"

At the shrill bellow of Cantonese, Glyn and Alan dropped their hands. "We were only having a bit of fun," they said sheepishly.

Low's father walked forward. "This is a private lane," he said in English. "What are you boys doing in it?"

The two boys backed away. "On our way home from school, aren't we?" said Al.

"We were only messing about," said Glyn. "We came up to see if Take – if Low was all right. 'Cause he wasn't in school. We saw your car and we thought—"

"—You thought you'd scare us both silly," said Wye Liew. He sounded irritated but Low had known him in bigger rages.

"Where Skiff?" asked Low in English.

"Oh, him," said Glyn.

"We're fed up with his big head," said Al.

"He's all right some of the time," said Glyn.

"He just gets a bit heavy," said Al.

"What happened the other dinnertime...we reckoned it was really good, how you...um..." Glyn dried up as he realized Low's father was listening.

"Stuck up for yourself," Alan put in. "We were thinking, could you show us all that Kung Foo stuff?"

Low laughed as Wye translated. "Whatever am I supposed to say to that?" he asked his father.

"I will suggest they find themselves some sort of martial arts club," Wye Liew replied.

Low listened to his father speak in English to Al and Glyn.

It's not so hard to understand, he thought as he picked out the words he knew.

"You coming back tomorrow?" Glyn asked Low.

"My son will be back on Monday," Wye Liew replied. "First, he has to visit the dentist."

Al and Glyn clutched their jaws and made moaning noises as Wye Liew shepherded his son away from them. "Aaarrrgh!" Glyn yelled. "Best-ta-luck, Low!"

Low bent his head to hide his smile, pleased at being called Low and at the good wishes. As the two boys headed down the lane his smile broadened into a grin of delight.

"It is good to have you home, Low," smiled Sau. "Do you feel completely well?"

Low was not sure how to reply. In his body he felt fine, but his mind was in turmoil.

"You must take it easy for the rest of the day," Sau went on. "Go and sit down and I will bring you some lunch."

Low went into the living room and collapsed

on to the cushions. Kitty came up to him and gave him a slimy wet yellow duck and an even wetter smile.

"Hello, Kitty," he said, ruffling her soft hair. He bent forward and gave her an experimental peck on one rosy cheek.

Kitty giggled. She pushed the duck at him. "Duck," she informed him, rushing off to find another toy.

"Oh no, not *that* game again," groaned Low.

"Right then," said Sau, coming in with a small tray. "Sweet and sour pork, rice and a can of Coke. Is that all right?"

"Mmm, lovely," said Low, sitting up. "Thanks, Mum," he added, trying out the new words in English. He took a mouthful of meat. "This is what everyone mentions, when they hear we've got a Chinese take-away," he told her. "They all say, 'Oh yes, sweet'n'sour!' You'd think it was the only Chinese dish!"

"It is a very important dish," Sau remarked. "It is like life itself. Sometimes, sweet things happen. Sometimes sour. A balance of the two gives the richest life."

She gave Low one of her smiles and glided back to the shop.

From its little alcove, the Buddha seemed to be staring down at him. Low chewed a piece of pork, and stared back.

"D'you know if Nanyang was a dream, fatman?" he asked, ungraciously. "Bet you do." His great-grandfather would have said that the Buddha knew everything, because he was at the heart of everything.

"Then you know what it's been like for me," Low went on, waggling his chopsticks. "Suffering here, suffering in Nanyang, oh yes, I know what it's like to taste the sour things in life, all right."

He took another mouthful of food. "It's about time I got something sweet," he told the porcelain statue above him. "Iz abou' bloomin' time," he added in English.

But the Buddha only continued to smile down on him, impassively, as if he hadn't heard a word.

CHAPTER TWENTY-FIVE

"OK," said Tristam. "You hold him, and I'll clean his cage." He scooped the furry creature up and handed it to Low. "Not scared, or anything are you?"

"Say again?" asked Low.

"Scared...um..." Tristam scratched his head. He kept forgetting that Low could not speak much English. He pointed to the hamster and then backed away, making little shrieks of terror.

Low laughed. "No scade," he tried. Scared of a hamster? If he'd had enough English, he might tell Tristam what scared him. Seeing the tin mine or the creaking junk in his head scared him. Looking down into the lane from his bedroom window scared him. Going to sleep scared him.

He held the soft, tan fur to his cheek. It reminded him of the flying squirrel he'd found last year, and of the dream he'd had...a dream within a dream...that was the sort of thing that scared him.

"I'll clean and you watch," said Tristam. "But next time it'll be my turn to hold Holland."

"Hol-lan'," said Low to the creature.

"Yeah, his name's a joke. Sean thought it up. But you wouldn't get it." He began to swill the hamster's treadmill in the classroom sink.

"Oh, look," Tristam went on, "there's that special teacher you get."

Sue Kung flew through the door of the unit in her sun-bird clothes. She was wearing baggy orange dungarees over which marched a procession of yellow teddy bears. A canary yellow blouse and bright yellow bootees completed her outfit.

She waved to Low. Somehow, the wave seemed urgent, and Low straight away dumped Holland into Tristam's hands. "I go," was all he said in explanation.

Sue was unloading her bag on to the table they used. "Low," she began in fast Cantonese. "I was in the library doing some study and I thought I might just see if there was ever a place called Nanyang." She drew out of her bag a piece of paper. "I photocopied this from an encyclopedia." She began to read:

"*Emigration was illegal, but Singapore-bound trading junks took Chinese coolies to work in the tin mines...*

In the nineteenth century the Malaysian peninsula was known as Nanyang.'"

She looked up. "I knew I was right. You did this as history, of course."

But Low hardly answered. He grabbed the paper and looked at the strange characters that made up English writing. If only he could read this! In one corner was a small black and white picture. A trading junk, sailing the high seas. His fingers slid over the familiar sight. On the ship's bow was painted the large, oval, all-seeing eye.

"What does 'emigration was illegal' mean?" he

asked.

"It means that people weren't allowed to go abroad."

Low nodded. "The Emperor would not allow it. You returned on pain of death."

"You see, you *did* learn all this at school," said Sue.

"Read it all to me," Low demanded. "All the page."

He listened as Sue read. In a few short paragraphs, the passage related the story of the tin mines and the emigrant coolies who were tricked into leaving their country to work in them.

"It doesn't tell everything," said Low, shaking his head. How could it? No one could imagine the terror, the exhaustion, the rationed food, the disgusting water, he thought, not unless you'd been there. Not unless you'd really experienced it for yourself.

A feeling of black foreboding took him over. His breath came in small gasps.

"Low, are you sure you're fit to be back at school? You don't look well."

"I'm fine," he lied. "I just want to forget about it."

"OK," said Sue, folding up the photocopied sheet. "Let's get down to work."

But I can't forget it, Low thought. I've just got to get it sorted out. And there's only one person who can help me do that.

Low was standing at a corner of the swimming pool, his toes curled round the lip of the tiles. Along from him, waiting in their lanes, were Tristam, Glyn, Alan and Skiff.

From the benches along the walls of the pool the rest of the Year Seven boys yelled their encouragement as a ragged row of swimmers splashed down the lanes towards the shallow end.

At the top of the pool, the five boys waiting for their turn stood in an electric buzz of malice that was being generated by Skiff and picked up by the others, as if they were TVs and he was the satellite dish.

"You wait, Take-Away," Skiff snarled at Low. "You are dead meat."

"Leave it, Skiff," said Glyn. "He's all right."

"Tell Skiff what his dad said," advised Alan.

"I'm not interested in what Take-Away's flamin' dad said," Skiff snapped. His rage found sudden expression. He bellowed his support to a flagging swimmer. "GET A FLAMIN' MOVE ON, MATTHEW!"

"His dad was saying about Kung Foo. Well, he said there's a club that does karate and things not far from here. Martial Arts, like."

"So?"

"So why don't we try it?" said Alan. "I wouldn't mind having a go at some of that stuff."

Skiff made a face. "You fancy having Take-

Away's foot stuck in your neck, do you?"

"OK, you horrible lot," said Mr Barrow, striding up the pool side. "I want these heats for the Swimming Gala sorted out today, not next year." He cast a glance to where Low stood quietly. "I hope there's not going to be a repeat of the trouble we had two weeks ago. Has that all been sorted out?"

"Yeah, it's all right now, sir," yelled Glyn.

"They're best mates now, sir," grinned Alan.

Low glared from beneath clouded brows down the width of the pool at Skiff, who stared sullenly back.

"When I blow my whistle, then, freestyle, OK, boys?"

"How's Low supposed to know what freestyle is, sir?" asked Glyn.

"He'll just have to catch on," said Mr Barrow, with a sarcastic smile.

When the whistle shrilled, Low watched as the other four boys sailed into the water. It took him precious seconds to realize he was taking part in a race. He dived off the side and slipped into a smooth, strong crawl. He didn't expect to overtake them now – he hadn't been one of the best swimmers in his old school – but at least he could try to catch them up.

He took a deep lungful of air and swam the second half of the length without surfacing for more. He touched the side and turned to see Skiff also splash in to touch the side.

They looked across the empty pool at each other. They were clearly the winners of their heat.

"You're flamin' fast, Take-Away, I'll say that," Skiff gasped. "I'm supposed to be the best swimmer in this year."

Low grinned and pushed his wet fringe out of his eyes.

"That's what I like, a nice bit of healthy competition," said Mr Barrow, kneeling above them. "OK, Low, you're in the school team as of Wednesday evening after school. Explain to him, will you, Skiff?"

"Brilliant swim, Low!" gasped Tristam, struggling up to the side and hanging on as he regained his breath. "I would've been third but I choked on some water."

"You always say that," said Alan.

The whistle went for the next heat. They all clambered out and grabbed their towels.

"Low's a winner for Littlecoot Comp!" yelled Tristam at some other mates.

"Just belt up, Tris," said Skiff. "You're getting up my nose badly. And listen to this," he added, turning to the others. "I'm flamin' s'posed to bring the Chinese Take-Away with me on Wednesday! Trust Barrow!"

Without meaning to, Low began to smile. He had clearly understood the gist of Skiff's words, and what was more, it occurred to him they sounded rather funny.

"P'hap you hungly, or somthin'?" he remarked.

"What?" demanded Skiff, skidding on bare heels

to face him.

The other four boys began to laugh.

"'E's got your number, Skiff," said Alan.

"Didn't you know he could understand what you say?" added Glyn.

"You take Chinese take-way 'cause you hungly," Low said, labouring his point. "Ve' nice food. But my name Low." He looked at Skiff with fire in his eyes, but kept the smile on his face.

Slowly, Skiff's mouth cracked into a begrudging grin. "Yeah. Ha ha. Very funny...*Low*."

Glyn put a wet arm round Low's wet shoulders. "Skiff'll be all right," he said. "He always is, if you give him time."

"That OK," said Low. "Plen'y time. I not goin' away."

CHAPTER TWENTY-SIX

"Low! Hey! Stop! Where are you going?"

Low spun round. Across the school playing fields, Henna was sprinting towards him.

"Hey, I haven't seen you for ages," she puffed as she caught up.

"I fell off fence. Hurt head."

"Low! You spoke English!" Henna broke into a wreath of smiles.

"I...ah...ho'pital," struggled Low. "An' after, I go dentist." He have her a fine grin, showing his drilled and filled teeth. Gold glinted in the weak afternoon sun.

"Gold fillings! Careful you don't get mugged!"

"Solly?"

"Only a joke." Henna fell in beside Low and walked with him. "Where are you going? This isn't your way home."

"On that road...ah...bu'top."

"You're catching a bus?"

"I go see my..." Low ran out of English and stopped dead.

"Um, friends?" hazarded Henna. And when Low shook his head, added as a wild guess, "Granny, or something?"

Low gave a massive nod. "House of Haw."

"Are you allowed? I mean, d'you know the way

back an' all?"

"My dad...ah...come...car."

"Oh, to pick you up." Henna giggled. "This is fun. I like crazy conversations. I'll walk with you to the bus stop, if you like."

Low summoned up all the English he could put together. He had news he was bursting to tell Henna.

"Ah... Miss Hale say...ah...I speak English gooder —"

"Better."

"Yeh. Better. Soon I in your class. First, I learn write English."

"Brilliant! I knew you'd do it!"

"English write easy," Low commented. "In Chinese, many letters."

"Yeah. You won't take long."

They stopped behind the small cluster of other Littlecoot pupils waiting for the bus.

"D'you know what to ask for, Low?" asked Henna, as a mini-bus came into sight.

"Solly?"

"What are you going to say to the bus driver?"

"Ah. Bis-tol cen-ter, piss."

"Pleeease," corrected Henna, smothering a smile.

Low climbed aboard, practising his pleases under his breath. Henna waited until he'd found a seat and then waved, hard. Low waved back.

It occurred to him that the last time he'd caught this bus he'd been confused, frightened, miserable and had not even cared if he was lost. He felt different now. Calm, more in control. Almost happy. But still confused.

Sue Kung had frightened him badly yesterday morning. When she'd read out the piece from the encyclopedia, the memories had all come winging back, as they did from time to time, even though he tried hard not to let them. They waited in the dark corners of his mind, looming up when he lost concentration at school or was watching the telly at home. At night, he lay awake until early dawn, and each time he nodded fitfully off he would jump awake again, an hour or so later, terrified and sweating.

Through the painful days of dental treatment, he'd begun to wonder about his great-grandfather. He always had an answer to a problem, it seemed. But it wasn't until Low had seen the eye of the junk staring out from Sue's photocopy that he'd finally made up his mind to go and see the old man.

"Don't pick me up from school tonight," he'd said to his father that morning. "I want to visit my honourable great-grandfather. I will go on the bus." He'd watched his father's face move into a expression of satisfaction and then into a smile.

How had Alan put it? He'd got his father's number – that was it. He had his number, at last.

The bus swung round a final corner and The House of Haw came into view. Practised now, Low pressed the button and the bus slowed as it came to the next stop.

A shudder of anticipation moved through his stomach.

Ly Ah Tang was Low's last hope – nobody else had listened to him. If Ly Ah had no answers, he would be left with the nightmare of his secret for ever.

Aunt Haw brought exquisitely patterned bowls of steaming tea. Low sat on the three-legged stool near the fire. Great-Grandfather sat erect in his chair and blew on the tea.

"Your father is well, Low Hee?" asked his aunt.

"He is well. He sends his greeting to you all," Low replied.

"And your mother, she is well?"

Low bowed his answer.

"And your sister?"

"Oh, Kitty!" grinned Low, no longer able to remain so formal at the thought of the irrepressible Kitty. "She's...well, she's just Kitty."

He watched his aunt lift the drink to the old man's whiskery lips.

"Go away," Low hissed silently at her, willing her to leave them, to go and work in the kitchen, or something.

"Low will help me with my tea," his great-grandfather whispered, as if he could read Low's thoughts.

Low bowed, and allowed his grandfather to sip

from the bowl. He sucked at the liquid with short little movements of his lips, like a rabbit sipping dew from grass stalks.

"I hear you have suffered an injury, my child," the ancient voice squeaked into Low's ear.

"I fell from the back fence," Low explained.

Ly Ah Tang licked tea from his whiskers. "Why was my great-grandson climbing the fence?"

Low took a long time to answer. He didn't want to go into details about the way he'd run away from serving in the shop. Then he realized that he didn't have to. Suddenly, he knew the real reason he had climbed the fence.

"I was looking for Liang."

"Did you find him?"

"Sort of. He...we...I found him floating in that blackness again."

What Low liked most about his great-grandfather was the way he gave Low time to think. He never hurried him for an answer, or interrupted, like most grown-ups. He let Low find the right words, however long it took.

"It happened when I fell from the fence. I blacked out. I could see myself lying on the ground. But I could see Liang too. Everyone is saying I just dreamed it," he blurted out, loud in his anxiety.

"I am not saying that," said Great-Grandfather.

Low plonked himself down on the stool, the bowl of tea still in his hands, and began to babble, getting everything muddled and in the wrong order.

Then, as he realized his great-grandfather would sit still and listen without interruption for as long as he needed, he calmed down, and began from the beginning, and told his tale through to the end.

"Now I'm afraid to go to sleep," he added. "I'm frightened I'll go back to that terrible place."

"You must not be afraid of sleep," said the old man, rocking himself in his chair. "I am sure you will not go back."

Low felt himself let out a tightly-held breath.

"Against all the probabilities," Ly Ah went on, "you and Liang attracted each other, over space and through time, like two ends of the same magnet. For a time that was outside time, Liang was a being without a home. He wanted his body back, but that was not possible. He'd lost the direction a soul should take. He searched around through space and time for something that felt familiar. And was drawn towards you."

Low felt strongly that Ly Ah might be right about them being magnetized to each other. Liang had always said he felt Low calling him.

"He found his direction in the end," said Ly Ah. "He went into the light. He has gone for ever, Low. You will never see Liang again."

"But how did it happen?" asked Low. "And why? Why should a boy who lived years ago be drawn towards me?"

"We are all on a wheel that will drive us round until we reach perfection," Ly Ah squeaked in his high voice. "That is what the Buddha taught."

Low nodded. "I know that we all live many lives. We live as many times as it takes to learn all the right thinking."

"The quest for a perfected soul is long and hard," Ly Ah said. "It takes many incarnations. Our bodies are only vehicles for our souls. When the body has aged, it has to die. Then, the soul must find a new vehicle. It might have been that Liang was attracted to your body because you shared the same soul."

"You mean—" Low could feel his breath tightening again, "that I was once Liang...that I am a reincarnation of him?"

"It might be so. We are all many reincarnations. Lifetime after lifetime. This is the Buddhist belief."

"No, I can't be Liang's reincarnation. Every life is lived better than the last. And all those years ago Liang was already a much better person than I am."

Liang had borne his pain and suffering without complaint. He'd worked hard each day without making any fuss. Above all, he'd kept quiet about the Ho family's escape, even when he'd been beaten.

"Liang is the sort of person I would like to be," said Low.

His great-grandfather chuckled. "Haven't we agreed, you and I, that Liang was searching for the light? His silver cord had finally lost its link with his body, and he was ready to go to his ancestors."

"He *did* go into the light!" Low almost cried out.

"He disappeared and the next thing I knew..."

"...The next thing you knew," Great-Grandfather interrupted for the first time, "was that you were inside the wrong body. It was not Liang who behaved in the way you so admire. It was you, for Liang was already dead." For a long time Low sat silently, trying to puzzle out what the old man was suggesting. He turned the bowl of cold tea around in his lap.

"Liang couldn't remember his past life. He had no memory of anything. Was that because only the body belonged to Liang? With me trapped inside it?"

"The workings of the cosmos are too complex for us to understand," said Ly Ah. "But maybe it was the great attraction you felt for Liang's lost soul that trapped you in Liang's broken body."

"It's weird," said Low, remembering. "But when I was in Nanyang I had a dream. And in the dream I was myself – I dreamt of things there that I couldn't explain then, because I couldn't remember being me." He felt an excitement well up in him. "Liang couldn't have dreamt about planes in the middle of the nineteenth century."

His great-grandfather nodded. "Liang's old memories were shut away in a part of your mind. Only in dreams could you bring them to the surface."

A slow grin spread over Low's face. "It was *me* on the junk," he almost whispered. "It was *me* in the mines. And not a dream but a...a..."

"A slip of time. Of a lifetime."

"But I'm not brave like that. I'm not at all brave, really," said Low.

"The Buddha would tell you that our experiences help to make us the person we are. The things you went through have strengthened you. That is the simple truth," said the old man.

"I know I feel differently now." Low struggled to find the right words. "It's like, I'd got all caught up with not wanting to be in England. I sort of got inside it, until all I could see was how awful England was.

"Then, when I woke up in hospital, it was the complete opposite. I was all caught up with the horror of the tin mines. I felt glad to be out of there. England...well, it didn't seem so bad, in comparison."

Great-Grandfather Tang was nodding his head. His bald head bobbed backwards and forwards, catching the red firelight. "It is not important, the place you live in," he said, almost under his breath. "Not as important as the way you live your life. Loving the people you live with brings contentment and peace."

Low thought of his grandmother. He had loved her, and loved her still. He thought more of her than anyone in the world. He knew deep in his heart that he always would. One day, he decided, he would go and visit her. That would be nice. Perhaps when he was old enough to travel alone. Maybe he could take Kitty with him. It was a lovely thought, something to keep hidden deep inside, something to keep him going.

The old man pulled his maroon cap on to his head and settled his chin on to his chest. "Does my great-grandson know now why he should not be afraid to sleep?" Low heard him mutter as his wet eyes closed.

"Liang pulled me towards his soul," Low recounted, wanting to get everything straight, "and somehow, I lived inside his old body until I fell down the mine shaft. So, now, both Liang's body and his soul are gone. And I am...back here."

"Now Liang has found the place of his ancestors, he will never call you towards this place called Nanyang again."

"I know that," whispered Low. Tentatively, he touched his great grand-father's folded fists. "And I know why my great-grandfather is not afraid to die."

The tea was as cold as tap water. Low stacked the two bowls and carried the tray out to the huge kitchens.

"We might have a restaurant like this, one day," he told Aunt Haw. "Or I shall, when I'm bigger. I'll call it...'The House of Tang'."

"Humph," grunted Aunt Haw. "We'll have to watch out for you, I can see. I think it's time I telephoned your father. It's growing late."

Low glanced at his watch and then out through the window. "How strange," he said. "It's still not dark outside."

"That is because of the English clocks," said Aunt Haw. "Did your honourable mother not explain about the extra hour of daylight?"

"She tried," admitted Low. "She said the clocks went forward an hour. I have trouble understanding that."

"From now on, the evenings get lighter and the days get warmer. You have never seen an English springtime, have you, Low? You will love it. It is the best time of the year."

Low thought about this. No, he decided, he was not quite ready to "love" the English springtime. But, sweet upon sour, it might be better than the English winter. And that would be something, at least.

Lions

Berlie Doherty

Street Child

Jim crept forward, invisible in the deep shadows, and stood, hardly breathing just inside the gate.

Jim Jarvis is a runaway. When his mother dies, Jim is all alone in the workhouse and is desperate to escape. But London in the 1860s is a dangerous and lonely place for a small boy and life is a constant battle for survival. Just when Jim finds some friends, he is snatched away and made to work for the remorselessly cruel Grimy Nick, constantly guarded by his vicious dog, Snipe.

Jim's gripping adventure is based on the true story of the orphan whose plight inspired Doctor Barnardo to set up his famous children's refuge.